The Romance Equation

Hampton Thoroughbreds

DIANE CULVER

Diane Culver

DEDICATION

This book is dedicated to "The Crew"
Ally, Ian, Kate, Mike and Paul

May they be successful, love life, live long, love math and
always, always use the proper "jargon".

CHAPTER ONE

Dulles Airport
Washington, DC
6 a.m.

Courtney Stockton peered out the small window of the Director's Lear jet. The black SUV, which had transported her to the private side of the international airport, backed up and drove away, its blue security lights no longer flashing. She tried to relax by leaning her head on the headrest of the beige leather seat. Exhausted and tired from having traveled nearly forty-eight hours with little to no sleep, she could barely keep her eyes open.

Eleven years ago, the job with the CIA had become her life. Not one to ever question her superiors, she inwardly admitted to herself she was pissed she'd been pulled from her current assignment in Positano, Italy. She'd spent two arduous years reeling in Salvatore Ponti, and now she was leaving, with him on the brink of confiding where the art work stolen from several major European museums was being sold on the black market. The information would allow the Agency to identify Sal's accomplices and track where the monies from the transactions were being diverted in order to fund ISIS terrorists in Syria and Iraq.

Glancing down at her watch, still set on Rome time, she wondered about the delay in taking off. Up to that point, everything had moved with precise timing in order to get her to the jet, which would carry her to New York City. Since the door to the cockpit was ajar, she could hear the pilot and co-pilot conversing through their headsets regarding the pre-flight check. Two flight attendants busied themselves about the small kitchen galley, seemingly not bothered at all by the delay.

She closed her eyes for a quick catnap, her mind wandering to the call from the CIA Director's office two days earlier. Courtney was shocked to hear Sam Tanner's voice on the other end of the line. Agent Tanner, the Director's second-in-command, had ordered her back to Langley *immediately*. There would be time later to ask questions. Doing as instructed, she'd packed her bags, briefed her team, appointed a new head of ops and jumped aboard the flight Sam had booked for her out of Rome. Despite the fact the Director had put a plausible cover story for her absence into place, Courtney worried Sal's ambitions stretched too far and wide globally. The man was a snake, one who could pop up in the most unusual and unexpected places.

Feeling a light touch on her arm, Courtney reached for her Sig Sauer pistol holstered under her jacket. As she did so, she opened her eyes to see a flight attendant staring down at her with a smile on her face.

Courtney withdrew her hand and placed it on the armrest, her trigger finger twitching. "Sorry, force of habit."

"No problem, Agent Stockton. Can I get you a beverage? Something to eat? I was informed no one gave you a chance to clean up. There's a washroom in the back to the right of the office."

Courtney could definitely use some nourishment, but she had to ask, "What are we waiting for? Why haven't we taken - "

The woman did not answer her question. Instead, she pointed out the window where Courtney had been staring earlier.

"We've been waiting for *him*." Courtney's eyes followed the agent's index finger and saw a line of three black SUVs, all with blue and red security lights flashing, moving toward the jet at a fast pace. "No doubt he was late leaving Langley."

Well. Well. Of course, he would have been. No doubt the Director had given him a list a mile long and added to it as he walked out of her office.

Courtney simply nodded in reply. "Well then, I'll take you up on your offer of food. Would it be too much trouble to see if there might be any Baileys stockpiled away? If there is, I'll take a liberal shot of the liquor in a large cup of coffee. No sugar."

"Baileys in your coffee?" Puzzled, the attendant replied, "Let me check."

As the woman turned toward the galley, a deep voice boomed out, "I see we're going to have to break you in, Agent Jacob."

Sam Tanner! Courtney stifled a chuckle. The man could sound extremely intimidating when he chose to. He took great delight when it came to dealing with rookie agents fresh from the Farm.

Agent Jacob stuttered, "Yes, sir!" The poor woman stiffened and stood at attention, her neck craning to look up at the tall man blocking the aisle. He was an imposing figure. In a way, Courtney felt sorry for the agent. She apparently must have drawn the short straw to get assigned the jet job. But from experience, Courtney knew the Director sometimes did things that had people shaking their heads later.

Sam pointed toward the kitchen. "Fourth cabinet on the right." In a gentler tone, he said, "And, please, I'll have the same."

When Agent Jacob finally made her way to the small galley, Sam plopped his large frame in the seat across from her, a wide grin on his face. "So how's the world traveler doing this fine morning? Hope you got some sleep coming across the pond."

Courtney crossed her arms over her chest and leveled a withering glare at him. "You know perfectly well I can't sleep on any kind of airplane. Do I look rested? I have bags under my eyes, and there are wrinkles in my suit. Look at me." She changed her tone of voice, flashing him an impish grin. "*If* I'd been able to fly first class, I might look a tad more presentable."

Sam chuckled while trying to accommodate himself more comfortably in his seat. "While you were in Europe, the President made budget cuts. Thank your lucky stars the Eagle pays for this plane out of her own pocket." He paused. By the expression on his face, he looked as if he was seeing her for the first time. "Gosh, it's good to see you, Court."

"It's good to see you, too, boss. I hate messaging with those encrypted cell phones and talking to you from local cafes via Skype." She winked, and he smiled in return. She'd forgotten how long it had been since they were in the same place. She eyed the man who'd been like a father to her when she'd abandoned her own. Sam's hair had turned snow white, but he still held his six-foot frame erect. Even at the age of sixty-two, his body hadn't lost its muscular tone. She'd bet her paycheck he put in twenty miles a day, either jogging or on a treadmill. The man put some of the younger agents to shame last May when he'd finished before them in the Army Ten Mile Race held in DC.

"Now, listen," Sam said. "We both need that jolt of caffeine and a bit of food. Things have gotten a bit mucked-up since we last spoke. I've got to get you up to speed before we land."

As if on cue, Agent Jacob appeared with two steaming mugs of coffee on a tray. When Courtney saw what else lay on a small plate, she extracted a seat-side table from the wall of the plane and unfolded it so she and Sam would have a place to eat.

"These are for you, Agent Stockton. Fresh chocolate chip scones with clotted cream."

Courtney took the white square plate. Her mouth watered at the sight of food. "Thank you. This is certainly a special treat."

"The Director said to enjoy. Mentioned something about London and tea. I didn't quite get the connection."

"Where's mine?" Sam questioned the woman.

"Oh, sorry. Yours is right here, sir." From the service tray, the woman placed a small bowl of oatmeal topped with golden raisins in front of him. "The Director said no scones for you. She said to tell you it was for your own good. If there's a problem you can call her."

Agent Jacob put the tray under her arm and briskly walked back to the galley.

Courtney should have waited to start nibbling on her breakfast. Caught trying to laugh over Sam's predicament and eat at the same time, she started to choke. She reached for her coffee to unclog the crumbs of scone lodged in her throat.

Sam grumbled, "That old battle axe never lets me have anything I want to eat anymore since the company doc gave us all physicals a month ago. Go ahead, girl. Snicker all you want." He stopped ranting and dove into his breakfast as if he hadn't eaten for days.

The old battle axe. Courtney smiled inwardly, recalling the Director. How many years had Agent Tanner and the Director worked side by side? He, the Black Swan. She, the Eagle.

Rumors swirled for years the two had an affair thirty-plus years ago while working a case in the European Theater. To this day, no one would doubt the deep respect and professionalism they showed one another, either at work or at any other function.

"Flight crew, ready for take-off." The pilot's voice came over the PA. "ETA is approximately fifty minutes. Temperature at JFK is 45 degrees."

Courtney licked her fingers, savoring the final crumbs before handing her plate over to Agent Jacob. Sam did likewise. Securing the tray table back into position, she buckled her seat belt.

Within minutes, the jet taxied down the runway. Courtney looked out the window just as the sun broke the horizon. She and Sam were making their first stop in New York City, but ultimately, she was going home - to Hampton Beach. A place full of memories. Some good, some bad. But, more importantly, she'd be coming face to face with the man she'd vowed never to see again.

* * *

"So, do you understand how serious the issue is and why the Director choose *you* to help deal with Thomas? After conferring with your brother, it was decided you're the only one who can get the job done." Leaning back in his chair, Sam crossed his arms.

Courtney surmised he was waiting for a sharp retort, but she needed time to digest the information about what had changed since they'd spoken two days ago. Finally comprehending their need for her to come back to the States now instead of later, she didn't have to like the idea. It was her job. She'd no choice but to comply.

According to Sam, her brother, Rick Stockton, CEO of

Stockton Investigative Enterprises, had merely skimmed the surface into the embezzlement at Hallock Farms. She and Sam were to meet him and his team in New York first. Then, they'd head out to Hampton Beach and the farm's main office in Southampton. Courtney had to admit she was stunned by the scope of what was happening, given what a tight ship Thomas, the CFO, typically ran. The man was and always had been a financial wizard.

Tapping her fingers on the armrests of her seat, Courtney spoke her piece, choosing her words carefully. "I fully understand the situation now, Sam, given the new facts. But I was to enter the operation as a closer only *if* my job in Positano had wrapped up. There are plenty of other agents with my background in forensic accounting who could do what needs to be done." Courtney drained the remnants of her cup and signaled to Agent Jacob.

"The same?" the agent asked.

"No. Just black this time. Sam? More for you?"

"Yes. Plain black with two liberal scoops of sugar."

Courtney could only shake her head as he winked at her. The man was impossible. He'd get his sugar fix somehow. She could only imagine what he'd stowed away in his carry-on bag to assuage his ever-present sweet tooth.

Sam continued, "From the moment Thomas called to detail what was transpiring, Rick had to contact the Director. The scope of the crimes committed needed more than the standard resources your brother uses. Rick also knew it was not going to be easy to keep Thomas in line as he and his team went on with the investigation. Even the Director tried to use her leverage as a Board member to get through to him. That's when she told me we had only one option - to bring you back home. Need I say, Rick was elated, knowing you'd be able to help out."

"Sam, the Director knows the history. I'm going to butt heads with the man the minute we see each other. I don't need to spell it out any further."

"No, you don't. But, this case is personal, and the Director has to be sure she distances herself. She has to be careful about crossing the line. Rick's running point. Come now, Court. We are certain you can remain objective, given what happened in the past. Thomas needs someone to answer to, keep him somewhat in the loop and calm him down when the going gets rough. That would be you."

Courtney snorted. "You think? Thomas is going to go ballistic. The only plus side so far is that I'll be seeing my brother. We haven't crossed paths in two years."

Out of the corner of her eye, she saw Agent Jacob approaching them, seemingly hesitant to break into their intense discussion. "Your coffees?" she asked.

Courtney took hold of the cup and blew on the hot liquid. Taking a sip, she jerked when it burned the roof of her mouth. Her mind had traveled elsewhere - back in time to eleven years ago. The most embarrassing moment of her life. The one that had sent her running from Hampton Beach to DC, to friends she could trust, and to begin a new life. Her thoughts at the time were to get as far away from Thomas as she could. Life obviously had other plans for her now.

"What's eating at you?" Sam placed his hand on her knee, his face awash in fatherly concern. "You're reliving that night, aren't you?"

Courtney sighed, placing her cup into the armrest holder. "My concern is my ability to maintain the necessary objectivity to work. I explained this to the Director. However, any way I spun it, I couldn't change her mind. She is hell bent on believing Thomas is going to listen to me and do as I say."

Sam's expression became serious. He leaned forward, his

elbows on his knees. "Courtney Ellen Stockton. You've never backed away from an assignment."

She could not look Sam in the eye so she glanced out the window of the plane. "This is *not* going to be easy for me. You know that."

"Copy that. Look at me." Courtney turned away from the window to see Sam eyeing her, his brow furrowed. "The Hallocks are as close to being family as you and your brother could possibly have. You, of all people, know how far back the relationship goes between your families. Yes, you're going to be tested in regards to your objectivity. But eleven years have passed. Hell, I've been in your shoes. The CIA trained you well, Agent Stockton. You wouldn't be sitting in that chair if the Director and I didn't think you could pull this off."

Courtney cringed at the subtle admonishment. Sam Tanner was the next best thing to having a father figure in her life. Her real father had been a drunk, a loser. A man who fell apart when her mother had died, leaving her and her brother and two sisters to fend for themselves. It had taken a while to trust Sam on a personal level, given the fact he was her boss, but she had gone to him often through the years on the job when she needed advice and support.

"What if I jeopardize this operation?" Courtney didn't realize until that moment how much self-doubt had built up inside her. It had to be coming from the thought of coming face-to-face with Thomas as the time grew closer.

"You won't. Trust me on this. The Director and I have your back. And besides, Rick is counting on you."

"But, Rick and I have never partnered up before."

"There's no one with a better set of skill sets to juggle the needs of two people than you. Hell, woman, you've headed up special ops for ages without blinking an eye. Don't tell me, now that you know what you know, you would have it any other way."

The PA system crackled. "Flight crew, prepare for landing."

Courtney shook her head, mulling over the comments Sam made and sighed. Her mentor was right. Family was family, whether related by blood or not. And the job was the job. One did as instructed.

Her biggest challenge awaited her. Should her brother be able to locate whoever was embezzling the money from Hallock Farm and save the company from imploding, it would be payback time. Didn't the saying go, "Whatever happened in the Hamptons stayed in the Hamptons?"

CHAPTER TWO

St. Regis Hotel
New York City
11:30 a.m.

Thomas Hallock glanced down at his Rolex watch as he sat at the bar of the prestigious New York hotel. The CFO of Hallock Farm noted only five minutes had passed since the last time he checked the dial. Frustrated and slightly annoyed with Rick Stockton, who had yet to arrive, Thomas drummed his fingers on the sleek wooden bar. Tardiness ranked right up at the top of the list of Thomas's pet peeves. Still, he'd known Rick since middle school, and the man in question was never late. *Never.* If he was, he always had a damn good reason why. The thought of Rick being a no-show shot a chill down Thomas's spine, especially with the deteriorating state of affairs he'd left behind in his hometown of Hampton Beach early that morning before getting on the company jet to New York City.

Thomas drained his glass of Scotch, caught the eye of the bartender on duty, and signaled for another. Normally, he made it a rule never to drink before five o'clock in the afternoon. He needed his head clear for the multitude of business tasks and decisions that came his way on a daily basis. But today was different. Desperate times called for desperate measures.

A little over a month ago, a simple five letter word surfaced during a routine accounting audit.

Fraud.

A slap on his shoulder, accompanied by the sound of a familiar voice, snapped Thomas from his musings.

"How long is it going to take for you to notice me standing here before you buy me a drink?"

Rick! His best friend and confidant had arrived.

Thomas moved to stand, but Rick indicated he stay seated. His friend's eyes roamed the room and then he parked in the adjacent stool.

Leaning in, Rick murmured, "Get ready to get the hell out of Dodge."

Taken aback, Thomas sputtered, "Come again?" Shaken up by Rick's command, Thomas barely noticed the bartender waiting.

Rick ordered a beer, but waited until the bartender was out of earshot before he spoke. "You've company, my friend. Contrary to what you may think, I'm not late. I've been here for well over an hour. I had a suspicion when I read over those notes you sent and got the call to meet you here, and not at your Southampton office, your every move would be followed. Four of my security men are doing surveillance in the lobby."

The bartender returned, but when Rick pulled out his wallet, Thomas brushed his hand away. "I've got this." He laid a fifty-dollar bill on the bar. "Keep the change."

The bartender did a double-take and looked at Rick, a broad grin breaking out on his face. "Thank you! Wish *my* boss was that generous." The man walked away.

"Thanks, Tom. I'll never hear the end of how my staff

could use a raise. He's one of mine."

Thomas glanced at Rick in disbelief. "I should have known. What else do I need to know?"

Rick nodded at the mirror behind the bar. "Two guys followed you in here. Rank amateurs, hiding behind their menus like I can't tell they're tailing you."

Thomas followed the path of Rick's gaze, his eyes falling on two men whose movements his friend studied suspiciously. One was large and burly, his biceps bulging underneath a black business suit, which didn't seem to suit his frame well. His hair, closely cropped to the sides of his head, was graying at the temples.

The other man immediately piqued Thomas's interest. Instinct told him he'd seen the younger man before. The second man's suit hung on his lanky body, his wire-framed glasses made him look like a teenager – a geeky, nerdy teen. Yes, there was definitely something familiar about him that rattled through Thomas's subconscious, but for now, he couldn't place him.

Rick sipped his beer, lowering his voice as he spoke. "Keep the conversation flowing in case there are others around. I need to think up a diversion."

In Thomas's book, Rick was the best there was. They'd shared a friendship for over thirty years, never losing touch after going their separate ways after college. Rick took his forensic accounting degree to Washington, DC where he worked for the FBI. Several years later, fed up with DC's bureaucracy, Rick left the job, taking some key, talented personnel with him to become CEO of one of the largest forensic investigative agencies east of the Mississippi: Stockton Investigative Enterprises.

Quietly sipping his drink with one eye on Rick, Thomas watched as his friend tipped his stool back, his eyes clearly fixated on the mirror.

Well, whatever he's looking at, I'll know soon enough.

Setting out to obey Rick's instructions of carrying on casual conversation, Thomas stated, "You're a hard man to get a hold of. Every call I made to that personal cell phone number you gave me went to voice mail. Care to explain?"

Rick signaled for another drink. The same waiter approached. "The same." This time he tapped three fingers on the bar in front of him as he placed his order.

"Got it. Be ready in just a few minutes." Thomas noted the man did not proceed directly to the mix station. The barkeep walked away with another order placed on a tray and made his way to the back of the restaurant.

Rick chuckled lightly. "It's kind of a funny story, actually. Your Aunt Elizabeth had me globetrotting all over the damn place. Paris, Athens, Rome, London. You name it, and I think my passport says I went there."

Curiosity got the better of Thomas. His aunt was the Director of the CIA. "Was she trying to recruit you to work for her again? That woman can be tenacious when she wants something…or someone."

His father's sister, having retired from life as an operative on the road, had spent the last eight years working for the current presidential administration as the Agency's Director.

Rick shook his head. "She sure as hell tried. She's persistent. I definitely can see a familial trait."

Thomas nodded. "All of us of Hallocks have that 'I won't take no for an answer' gene." He noted Rick suddenly pointing his head at the door that led to the main lobby. The duo would be on the move momentarily.

"What happened to our drinks?" Thomas asked. He desperately felt he needed one more for the road.

"Behind us, with that table of yahoos," Rick responded.

"Bernie went to block their lines of sight. Right now, he's screwing up their order. Go... *now.*"

Thomas threw another fifty-dollar bill on the bar and followed Rick, walking briskly to the nearest exit. "Ah, Rick? I didn't valet my car. I told the driver to take a break, and I said I'd call."

"You - never mind." The perturbed look on Rick's face spoke volumes. "Let's get the hell out of here."

Grabbed by his coat sleeves, Rick dragged Thomas past a stunned concierge. Standing at the curb, Rick muttered something unflattering under his breath. He hailed the first taxi that came down East Fifty-fifth Street. When the cab pulled up, Thomas opened the back door. Rick's hand pushed him hard from behind, sending him tumbling onto the seat. He landed off-balance with Rick practically landing in his lap.

"Go!" Rick hollered to the cab driver.

"Do you think they followed us?" A tinge of panic rang out in his voice. With his stomach tied in knots, he could barely speak.

Rick gave the cab driver an address Thomas knew all too well. "Not that I can tell. But I'd bet there's a strong possibility those two did not come alone."

Thrown back into his seat from the cabbie putting the pedal to the metal, Thomas tried to remain upright while the cab weaved its way into the heavy New York City traffic.

* * *

"Please tell me you've got that damn thumb drive."

Thomas pulled the requested item out of his jacket pocket and passed it off. He reiterated for his own piece of mind, "You got the documents?"

"Yes," Rick replied. "I looked over the copies you sent in

the overnight mail and forwarded them on to my guys. This is more than a simple case of fraud, Tom."

As the cab wove in and out of traffic, barely stopping for red lights, Thomas noticed Rick looking out the back window.

Rick rapped on the partition separating the cabbie from his passengers. "Step on it! I think we've got company. There's a couple hundred extra in your tip if you lose that black Town Car!"

The cabbie looked in his rearview mirror, muttered something unintelligible and stepped on the gas. The cab lurched forward, picking up speed.

Thomas's eyebrows shot up. "More? What do you mean 'more'?"

"I don't know the exact specifics. My team's been hard at work examining what you gave us. It's why I needed this thumb drive with the PDF spreadsheets."

"Your poker face isn't what it used to be, my friend. It's worse. Isn't it?" Thomas's heart rapidly pounded in his chest. The fast car ride wasn't the only cause of his anxiety and panic. The unknown of what was going down at Hallock Farm had him clenching his fists tightly together in his lap to steady his nerves.

Rick turned and stared directly at him, no longer scanning the scenery flashing by the cab's window. "You're not missing thousands, Tom. My best IT guy started going through the emails, tracking IP addresses. Those new computer systems you installed were royally compromised to the point where someone hacked directly into your financial accounts."

Thomas didn't know whether to be relieved or enraged that his suspicions were confirmed. But even with numbers being his thing, he'd known something was exponentially askew. His biggest fear was the culprit was someone within the Hallocks' inner circle. Warily eyeing Rick, he braced himself and asked,

"How bad?"

Rick waved the coveted thumb drive. "If this confirms what we already know…"

"Just spit it out!" Thomas grew impatient for answers. He wanted Rick to get to the point. Give him some idea of where this debacle was heading.

Rick tucked the drive inside the breast pocket of his navy blue blazer, then placed a hand on Thomas's arm.

"Three million is missing." Rick paused too long. Thomas's sixth sense told him more was to come. He held his breath. "That's just from one account."

Like a quarterback who'd been sacked, Thomas had the wind knocked out of him. Bile rose in his throat. Sweat broke out on his brow. He sat staring out the front windshield in a stupor, the nightmares that had plagued him over the last few days flashing through his mind. The "what-ifs" were coming to fruition. This wasn't a dream. Reality had sucker-punched him.

Three million plus! What explanation could he give to appease his family, the Board of Directors and the many stockholders he had to answer to? Six months ago, everyone trusted him to choose a new CEO to replace his sister, Kate. She decided to vacate the position she'd held since taking over the reins of the farm from their father, Robert. When Thomas met former Special Agent John Clinton, there was little doubt in his mind Kate was ready to give up all she'd worked hard to accomplish in Hampton Beach to follow the man she loved. Kate was now married and living a new life in Virginia, running Clinton Stables with her newly retired husband.

Thomas hired the best man for the job. Or so, he thought. Jack Jessup was a man whose family's roots went back to the Revolutionary War and the Battle of Long Island. The Jessups were "old money" and held in high regard. Jack attended

Hampton Beach High School with Rick and Thomas, graduating in a later class from Wharton. He'd done a successful stint on Wall Street. He was a solid hire, vetted by Rick and his aunt. The entire family had given him the thumbs-up.

Now what would happen to everyone involved with a stake in the farm's financials? Most depended on the income from the farm's dividends to contribute to their affluent lifestyle and business ventures. He sensed things would go from bad to worse before the night ended.

The stress mounted by the minute. Thomas inhaled and exhaled deeply. His pulse pounded rapidly underneath his skin, like a horse's hooves going headlong for the finish line.

The one, and only one, good thing Thomas could count on was the man sitting next to him vigorously texting an unknown source. Rick Stockton was a specialist in weeding out corporate fraud and espionage. His friend spent a great deal of time building his company to specialize in embezzlement cases. He thanked his lucky stars his best friend was the right man for the job. Rick would have Thomas's back. He always did.

CHAPTER THREE

Hampton Coffee Company
Southampton
Noon the same day

Janie Walker scanned the length of the line of people waiting at the counter then looked at the clock on the wall. She definitely had time to get her latte fix and wolf down a chicken salad sandwich. When Sammy, steadily working the crowd of the coffee shop, was free, they'd be able to talk. It was imperative, with so many people milling about, they make their lunch "date" seem real to those gathered around them. Neither she nor Sammy had a particularly good reputation in one of the Hamptons' finest communities. Several brushes with the law, recently played out in the headlines of the local paper, had people eyeing her warily as she waited to place her order.

Finally at the front of the line, she called to Sammy. "You going to be able to take your break?"

"Yeah. Give me five. Find a place to sit."

Janie nodded in the direction of an empty table by the window that looked out onto the main highway into town.

"I'll grab that one."

"Miss….Miss…" Another clerk snapped his fingers, glaring at her over the glass case where the pastries were displayed. From the look on his face, he was clearly annoyed.

"Sorry," Janie apologized. "I didn't mean to hold up you up. I'll do a mocha latte and this sandwich."

While the clerk made her beverage, Janie spied him eyeing her up and down. He wasn't the only one in the shop doing so. Even dressed in a dusty, heavy jean jacket, flannel shirt, denim overalls and work boots, Janie knew her natural beauty would make any warm-blooded man in the shop give her a once-over. With what she'd been assigned to do in the next few days, Janie knew her looks would work to her advantage.

With her order in hand, she reached the cash register where a teenager stood, smacking her gum. Punching a few buttons into the store's computer screen, the girl stated flatly, "That'll be six dollars and eight-nine cents."

Janie paid her tab, grabbed her order and walked through the swath of tables filled with people. Several glanced at her as she walked by. *Great. Just great.* This plan of Sammy's, "pretending" they were a couple, had better work. Janie hadn't wanted to meet Sammy to discuss their business at the busy Hampton Coffee Company. She'd have preferred a more isolated spot to get together. However, since her photo had been plastered all over the front page of the *Southampton Times* several months ago, there had to be several people who'd know who she was and what she had done. One thing "townies" in the Hamptons loved to do was commiserate about the elite crowd, or people who seemed out of place, especially since most led a solitary life from Labor Day to Memorial Day. And if you'd done something to get yourself in front of the local courts, they'd let you know they knew who you were. She couldn't wait to accumulate enough money to get the hell off Long Island.

"Sorry. Didn't think it would be this crowded. I don't have much time."

Janie stopped daydreaming as Sammy slid into the metal retro chair across from her. He popped open a can of Coke and unfolded a turkey toasted panini from its wrapper. After taking a few gulps of his beverage and eating several large bites from his sandwich, Sammy took a folded napkin out of his pocket. He hid it in the palm of his hand and reached across the table. He placed it in her hand, folding her fingers around it. He squeezed her hand tightly to give the impression to anyone nearby they were simply boyfriend and girlfriend meeting for a quick lunch date.

But certainly not by choice, Janie thought to herself.

"Time and place?" Janie asked, keeping her voice low. She eyed Sammy skeptically, still not sure what to make of the man she'd been paired with.

"Yup. The break-in is on. I can't believe those two stupid underlings didn't think we'd hear what they plan on doing. Janie, they managed to get hold of the master key. "

"How the fu...?" Janie's eyebrows shot up. "Who...?"

Sammy gave her a look that silenced her. He let go of her hand and reached for her chin, forcing her to look him directly in the eye. No one sitting nearby would suspect, by the way he held her, that they were planning their next move, especially when he stroked her cheek. Janie could barely keep her body from flinching at his touch. But she'd been given no say in the matter. There was just something about the man sitting across from her that had her wondering what his true motive was in the context of things to happen.

"Are you absolutely sure," he leaned over the table and whispered, "that you're going to have the necessary back-up?"

Janie sighed, brushing his hand from her face. "You worry way too much. I've got this. I'll be fine."

"I've been worried since we got involved in this."

Janie sat back in her chair and folded her arms over her chest. She was direct in what she said next. "Do I have to remind you we made a deal?"

Sammy's eyes pierced her own. "My take is we made it with the Devil. If you get into trouble, I can handle him."

"And you think *I* can't? Need I remind you which one of us got us the 'get out of jail free card' in the first place? There'll be plenty of protection for me…and you."

"Sammy!" A loud voice called out from behind the counter.

Janie saw Jake, the manager of the coffee shop, pointing at the clock. Time was up.

As Sammy pushed back from the table, Janie stood up, picking up the remnants of their lunch. She looked around for a waste can and spied one by the front door.

"Sammy! Back to work!" the manager barked again.

"I'm coming!" Sammy turned to her. "Geez, the guy never cuts me a break."

"I'll talk to you tomorrow. I gave you that burner phone. Be sure to use it."

With Sammy back behind the counter waiting on customers, Janie opened the door of the shop. She eyed the apple croissants in the display case. No, she thought. No time for a treat. She had a plan to map out and contacts to inform. She headed to the parking lot. With luck, she would be closer to a better life once her part in the deal with the District Attorney's office was put to rest.

CHAPTER FOUR

The yellow cab darted through the streets of Manhattan on its way from the Upper East Side toward its final destination: the Red Lion Pub on Bleecker Street situated on the Lower West Side. It was going to be one hell of a cab fare, given the promised tip.

Looking through the cab's front windshield, Rick saw the red-brick, four-story building on the corner. He took one last look over his shoulder. No black Town Car.

"Stop here," he called to the driver. The cab slowed and slid up to the curb.

Rick jabbed Tom in the ribs to get his attention. For the last ten minutes, his friend had sat in stony silence looking blindly out the window.

"Pay the man," Rick directed his companion. Without a thought, Thomas reached into his wallet and pulled out a wad of hundred dollar bills, flinging four of them at the driver. Rick scrambled out of the cab with Thomas right behind.

"Were we followed?" Thomas inquired.

"No. The Town Car's gone. Come on. Let's get inside." Grabbing Thomas by the elbow, Rick aimed him in the direction of the corner tavern. As the cab pulled away, Rick did his due diligence once more to look up and down the street. Starting to walk at a brisk pace toward the Red Lion, he said, "I called Joe while you were daydreaming. Told him to set up the back room. I also talked to two of my best people. They'll be here within the hour."

It didn't take long for both men to make their way inside the well-known eatery. The lunchtime crowd was still in full swing, the place buzzing with conversations. Irish music came through the sound system in the main dining area. ESPN and several local New York news channels played on the five large flat screen TVs, which hung over the bar. The place was packed.

"Rick! Tom!" Rick heard a thick Irish brogue call to them over the cacophony of noise. Joe MacAllister. He spied a man waving a white bar towel in the air to catch their attention. Joe had been a fixture at the pub for as long as Rick could recall. Joe came out from behind the bar and weaved his way through the crowded tables to greet them. "How are my boys?"

Upon the appearance of their old friend, Thomas rallied. The sullen look on his face vanished, replaced by a grin that went from ear to ear. "Joe! By God, it's good to see you."

Rick watched as the two men embraced. Tom towered over Joe. But what Joe lacked for in height, he made up for in his physique. Shorter and muscular with a military build, Joe had boxed in younger days. But his missions with the Agency forced him to remain in good physical condition, even to this day. Seeing Tom looking pleased and relieved, albeit temporarily, Rick knew the Director had pegged it right to make for the Red Lion. Joe had the connections that would aid Thomas during the farm's crisis. Joe would be the operation's eyes and ears on the ground in New York City and the perfect "go-to" agent between Rick and the Director.

"Joe? Can we take this reunion elsewhere?" Rick scanned

the crowd, a tinge of paranoia setting in that someone would recognize them. He nodded toward the back of the cordoned-off part of the restaurant. "Is the room ready?"

Joe called to his bartender. "I'll be right back." He pointed at three men sitting with their heads down at the end of the bar. "Watch them."

The barkeep shook his head in the affirmative and did as he was told.

"Follow me, lads." Joe walked off, a small limp in his step, weaving through the tables. Rick and Thomas trailed behind.

Rick had trouble trying to hear what the older man was saying with all the chatter. He tapped Joe on the shoulder as they made their way to the back of the tavern. "Say again?"

"Everything's all set. Ye'll have plenty of privacy," Joe replied. Arriving at the door off the large dining area, Joe asked, "Will ye be wanting something to drink?"

A drink seemed like a good idea, but Rick would have to keep an eye on Thomas's intake. He needed his friend focused.

"Sounds good," Rick replied. "I'll do a Guinness. Tom?"

"Ah, sure." Thomas's reply was devoid of any of his previous enthusiasm. And why shouldn't his emotions be on a roller coaster? The man's world had been turned upside-down. Hell, for all Rick knew, Hallock Farm and everything associated with the business could go belly-up if he and his team couldn't find out the truth ASAP. His gut told him that wasn't going to happen so fast. But he had great faith in the team he'd assembled.

A slap on the back refocused him to find Joe cheerfully exclaiming, "Beers it is. Ye'll let me know when ye might be wantin' something to eat. Shepherd's pie is the specialty of the house tonight."

Anxious to be out of the way of prying eyes, Rick pulled at Thomas's sleeve. "Let's make ourselves comfortable while we wait." He opened the door, and Tom entered the back room. Rick called to Joe, "You know who's coming."

Joe acknowledged the comment with a mini-salute. He walked off, disappearing behind the polished wooden bar.

Inside the room with the door shut, Rick steered Tom to one of the pub-style chairs at the end of a long, rectangular wooden table. A dartboard hung on the wall, all set up and ready, awaiting the players of a new game. The room looked as if it were prepped for a party. Sadly, there would be no celebration tonight. Candles flickered on the tables, and the dim light from the sconces on the walls gave off an eerie glow.

Hearing the click of a door opening, Rick turned, but was disappointed to see Kevin, a member of Joe's waitstaff. Kevin carried two beers on a tray and placed the glasses in front of them.

"Would you be needing anything else?" Kevin inquired.

Rick shook his head. "No."

"Joe said to text if you need anything. He'll check in when he can." Kevin walked to the door, opened it and walked out, leaving Rick to ponder the myriad thoughts running through his head.

Rick never pitied clients, even those who'd personally created their own trouble, prompting them to seek out his services. As a master investigator in the States and known internationally, he was paid exceedingly well for what he did. He and his team sought out the facts, worked to get the job solved and moved on. At the moment, the company had more work than it could handle. But *this*? This job wasn't just business. It was personal. As soon as he'd been contacted and learned the Hallocks were involved, he dropped everything, leaving the rest of his cases with his assistants. Rick was focused on Thomas and the rest of the clan who, in essence, were family. Rick was determined to bring closure to the case by helping in whatever way he could.

The dejected look on Tom's face gnawed at Rick's gut. Thomas had removed his jacket, rolled up his shirt-sleeves and loosened his tie. Swallowing a large swig of beer seemed to ease the pained expression on his face. Never could Rick remember a time when he'd seen Tom this low. Rick's primary job was to get to the truth and convince his friend to get ready for the fight of his life if he wanted to save his family legacy. The pressure was unlike anything he'd ever experienced. Everything rode on his firm uncovering the fraud ring that had developed practically overnight.

Rick watched Tom's body language for a clue to talk.

It was Tom who spoke first. "Wipe that look of pity off your face. You have no idea of my rage right now. I'm wracked with guilt." Tom jabbed his forefinger at Rick. "Tonight, don't you dare lie to me or gloss things over. I've got people to answer to. I need to be able to tell them how we're fixing the issue to recoup their money—if that's even a possibility."

For the first time since the day their friendship began, Rick was at a loss for words. From the communications he'd received up through this morning, he knew only the broad scope of details of the scam infiltrating Tom's main office in Southampton. When his two men arrived, Rick had a feeling things were going to spiral downhill if he and his team didn't handle the situation by being logically direct. In Tom's world, if A equaled B and B equaled C, then A *better* equal C, which meant his company had to deliver.

Rick drew in a deep breath and put his hand on Tom's arm, a simple gesture he hoped Tom took as reassurance. "I swear to you I won't sugarcoat anything, but your aunt's been in touch with my IT men. She says, 'It's bloody bad'."

Tom took another liberal swallow from his glass. "Where the hell is this team of yours? I'm sitting here on pins and needles. Tell me whatever you can. I'm not about to make idle chit-chat. I won't interrupt. I swear." He made the sign of the cross over his heart. "You talk. I'll just drink."

Rick ran his hand through his dark hair. He was as frustrated as Tom. "I only know the basic framework. This is all happening so fast. What I know comes from my team working round the clock doing research."

Tom's white-knuckle grip on the handle of his now empty mug was Rick's clue Tom wanted in-depth answers. Where *were* his IT guys? Rick wanted his ducks in a row and all the data placed in front of Tom. He wasn't used to meeting with a client to discuss the merits of the case without details. Should he make a phone call? No. Since he'd picked up Tom at the hotel, he'd worried his GPS was being tracked.

Before Rick could tell him to turn off his phone, Tom's fist suddenly slammed onto the tabletop. Rick jumped, taken off-guard. His friend's face was red, his brow furrowed. Tom looked at the closed door.

"Want another beer?" Anything to appease Tom as the clock on the wall, its pendulum swinging back and forth, reminded him of a ticking time bomb.

A commotion came from the doorway. Turning to look, he released a huge sigh of relief. Andrew and Troy, his best IT specialists, entered the room. Now he'd have the updated information that should, he hoped, put Tom in a better state of mind. Anything new his team uncovered would allow Rick the chance to ramp the operation into high gear. It was imperative a plan be laid out for the recovery of the stolen money. He prayed the two, along with others on the investigative team, had been able to work their magic.

Rick and Tom stood as the two men advanced toward them. "Andrew and Troy will be coordinating all levels of the investigation regarding your computer network. Meet Andrew

Martin, my firm's number one forensic accountant."

Thomas's face showed a look of relief that matched his own. He shook Andrew's outstretched hand and reached across the table to acknowledge the other man's.

"Troy Dillion." The man with the tortoise shell glasses introduced himself.

Rick wanted Tom to know the role each would play in the ensuing days. "Troy is the master guru of computer programming, one of the best IT hacking men in the world. There isn't a system the man can't get into."

"Since I'm paying top dollar, I'm counting on the best of the best getting my money back." Tom warily eyed all three men and sat back down. He stared up at the two men whose gazes darted from Rick to Tom and back again. "If I don't sound grateful for all you're doing, I'm sorry."

Rick, still standing, shoved his hands in his pockets. "No need to apologize." Rick pointed to Andrew and Troy. "Sit down and get set up. You need to brief us, obviously. You've got two hours."

Out of the corner of his eye, he spied Joe standing in the doorway. He hadn't heard the man enter with all the commotion. Rick motioned for Joe to come forward, but the man didn't move.

Joe eyed everyone and asked, "You ready for dinner?"

Seeing his men engaged in setting up their laptops and Tom merely staring at the table in a zombie-like trance, Rick took the liberty to order. "Four beers and some of that pie should do just fine. We've a long night ahead." Rick wearily smiled at the older gentleman.

"Coming right up." Joe critically eyed Thomas, jerking his head in his direction. "Should I keep the beverage flowing for that one?"

"No." Rick replied adamantly. "I want him coherent and

alert."

When Joe exited the room, Rick turned back to the assembled group and slid into the chair next to Tom. "Lay out what you found. Major decisions have to be made based on what you've brought to the table...*tonight*."

CHAPTER FIVE

Thomas heard the snapping of fingers and realized he'd drifted off to think about everything going on around him over the last few weeks.

Rick asked, "You ready?"

"Go for it."

Andrew and Troy pulled a stack of papers out of each of their respective laptop bags as Troy booted up the thumb drive in the USB port of his computer.

"Andrew, start with your preliminary findings. Ground zero. What'd you two dig up?" Rick asked.

Andrew spread out a series of color-coded papers. "We started by scrutinizing those invoices Mr. Hallock sent. Then cross-checked data between what was listed on the farm's office databases in Southampton and the numbers from the originals he'd stored in his safe."

No matter how many computers, iPads, iPhones or other advanced hardware are housed in the main office, thank God I insisted on having paper copies of everything.

"Was I right?" Tom perked up in his chair. He looked directly at Andrew, but said nothing else.

"Yes. You were spot on with your suspicions. There were

huge discrepancies. Not only with the invoices, but, as Rick has informed you, we started finding monies transferred out of accounts. There is no evidence the money was swapped from one account to another for a business transaction. No notations. The money is gone."

Thomas's heart pounded in his chest. His hands trembled, and he braced himself for the reality about to set in. "Rick mentioned only one account."

"I don't work on assumptions, Tom," Rick interjected. "What I told you was the information I had at the time. Andrew and Troy are going to map out everything they've pieced together."

Thomas played with the handle of his empty mug. He wanted to take control of the meeting, but had to leave it to Rick. "How much, Andrew? Rick said three million. That was at noon. You just mentioned *accounts*. Plural means a hell of a lot more."

Knowing Rick's top men for less than thirty minutes, Thomas sensed Andrew's and Troy's unease. He was sure Rick had instilled in his staff just how important Hallock Farm was as a client, a very high profile client. Andrew, who'd done most of the talking thus far, seemed to be a consummate professional, precise and to the point. Thomas liked the fact the man was direct and straightforward.

Andrew glanced down at the screen of his laptop. "Mr. Hallock, transfers have totaled seven million dollars."

He appreciated the young man getting right to the point. *No doubt he realizes the severity of what I'm up against.* Thomas clenched his fists at the news, then folded his hands, interlocked his fingers, and placed them on the table.

Troy spoke up, adding to the information Andrew had imparted. "Quite honestly, whoever started this scam was pretty stupid. Finding the pattern of withdrawals from the accounts was fairly straightforward. There's a definitive pattern.

Transfers always occurred when certain investors bought thoroughbreds *or* paid for certain farm services. Based on your invoices' spreadsheets, coupled with what your clients paid, I can see exactly how monies were skimmed from the accounts and transferred to dummy accounts invested elsewhere.

"The team's concern is your farm income is invested in a variety of funds, several large ones established when Katherine Clinton began her equine training center. We've attached red flags to each one. With all due respect, someone should have monitored those more carefully. We're going to need access to the list of people who work in the office now and those you've previously employed."

Thomas heaved a weighty sigh and nodded. From years in the business, he'd been knee-deep in fighting with his father, Robert, the family patriarch, over the bills that piled up. His father had served as CEO before Kate had taken over. The man had no business acumen and, unbeknownst to the family, had accumulated friendships with several unsavory partners. That had left Thomas and Kate to right the wrongs of the farm's affairs. And here he was doing it again. The word "fraud" somehow didn't fit the situation. What was going on was on a far grander scale.

Andrew broke in. "We found you also acquired investments last year when you bought into the ownership of several thoroughbreds at Clinton Stables. Your sister and her husband are the main shareholders of their stables, true?"

Tom nodded. *Where was this going?*

"My findings show your company owns a twenty percent stake in the new farm as part of its portfolio."

Thomas blanched, his eyes widened. "Are you telling me Kate and John are in jeopardy of losing money, as well? Damn it! Kate poured her heart and soul into our farm. Rick, you know very well what she went through when she took over from Father! How am I going to explain to my new CEO, Jack Jessup, who signs off on monetary matters on my say so? Everyone relies on my expertise when I invest monies. Good God, how could I have been so blind not to realize this?"

"With all due respect," Andrew said. "Any CFO can't see the entire financial picture all the time. That's why you hire supposedly well-trained CPAs for your staff. Personally, sir, my take is, this is an inside job."

"But—"

Rick, who'd said very little up to that point, interjected, "Tom, let Andrew and Troy finish."

Thomas buried his head in his hands. "When this hits the newspapers, they'll have a field day. The last thing the farm needs right now is this kind of publicity. It's the height of the buying season! We'll lose clients left and right. The people who entrust their horses to us for training will be thinking, if we can't manage our business, we can't properly take care of their horses."

"You may need some help from members of the Board who have deep pockets," Rick replied. "There are several I know who will quietly aid Andrew and Troy once we've explained what the plan is. Those with close ties to your aunt will definitely be a financial asset should we need them."

Thomas rose from his chair and paced the room. He stopped only to massage the back of his neck with his hand. The tension in his head had built to the point where he could feel a migraine coming on. Bringing his hands to rest at his waist, he took a defiant stance in front of the three men who sat watching his every move.

In a commanding tone, Rick said, "Sit down."

"I can't think sitting down. I think better on my feet," Tom countered.

"I'm not giving you a choice. The longer you drag this out

and I don't get all the facts to strategize, the longer time it takes to get to Southampton and finish this once and for all." Rick pointed to the chair beside him. "Park your ass in the chair. *Now.*"

Thomas heeded Rick's instructions. He turned to Andrew. "Where do you suspect the money went?"

"We have a few leads. Right, Troy?" The man to Andrew's right simply nodded and kept scrolling through the spreadsheets on the computer screen, jotting notes on a pad of paper. "Monies are being siphoned from almost every account we've been able to access. That's where things get complicated."

Both Thomas and Rick looked at one another.

"Define 'complicated'," Rick bit out.

"Whoever's behind this hack job went in and changed the passwords protecting some, not all, of the programs in your new computer system. It allowed *them* access while keeping anyone who works for you out. We're working hard to break the encryption to get over their firewalls. That part is definitely the work of a pro."

"But you said you thought there's a good possibility it's an inside job?" Thomas countered, perplexed. "How on earth is that possible? We're as locked down and secure as possible. I paid for the best system out there."

"Ah…" Andrew seemed to want to add something but was hesitant to do so.

"Go ahead, Andrew. Speak your mind." Rick pushed the conversation forward, for which Thomas was grateful. Sweat was starting to pour from his brow. "Lay what you think right on the table."

"Sir, with all due respect, I just can't fathom why one of those CPAs did not bring this to your attention."

"How long do you estimate it's been going on?" Rick asked in a rougher voice than before.

"The perp probably let the staff get comfortable with the new software, which wouldn't take long with good training. Then based on their data inputs, he found the right times to hack in. Anyone with computer encryption training knows there are ways to control computers without being detected. It's easy to fake the books internally from that point. I've managed to trace the origins of the first few transfers back through the network of your office's computers. Whoever started this process left a small cyber trail. Troy and I need access to everyone's laptops, computers, tablets and phones for business and personal use. But that raises the issues of obtaining search warrants."

"But they're my computers." Thomas was confused.

Andrew smiled. "Not for those that belong to the company. For those used personally by the staff. The scope of this job is far-reaching. The invoices were a good starting point. Good thing you're old school."

Thomas knew Andrew was trying to add a bit of levity to the night. He began to pound one fist into the palm of the other, his mind on a mental image of smashing the living crap out of the first person found along the cyber-trail who had anything to do with what had transpired.

Andrew cleared his throat. "Rick, we're going to have to pull in a number of resources from the Agency, the FBI and the DOJ."

Thomas's head snapped up. "The DOJ? What for?"

"With their cooperation, we can expediently obtain the necessary warrants for wiretaps, cell phone records, bank account transactions. The team has no doubt this case has gone international."

Troy, who had been scanning document after document on the screen of his laptop, cut in. "There's a ninety-nine percent chance the monies have already been funneled outside the US borders to off-shore accounts. The Caymans, Swiss accounts and other European banks, you name it."

Thomas shuddered and took a deep breath. He prayed he wouldn't start hyperventilating and develop a panic attack in front of everybody. As it was, he felt cold and clammy from anxiety.

"Tom, you okay?" Rick reached out a hand to grasp his arm. "I *promise* you, we'll apprehend whoever the hell did this."

"What exactly is your plan?" A slight slur indicated the alcohol he'd imbibed had started to affect his speech. "I need another beer. Where's Joe?"

"No. No more," Rick stated firmly. "You've got to have your head in the game."

Like a leprechaun, Joe appeared from out of nowhere, bringing not only a beer, but a shot of Grey Goose. Thomas drained the shot glass *and* the pint of ale before Joe had time to leave the room. Rick, Andrew and Troy stared at him, wide-eyed.

Amid the buzzing in his brain, he tried to speak slowly and succinctly. "You don't... have much... t – t - time. I've got a meeting with my...my... board in three days. I have to—" He slumped back into the leather pub chair.

Suddenly, someone shook him by the shoulders. He focused his blurred vision on Rick's angry face. "Don't fade on us now! We came up with an idea."

"Don't keep me waiting. Tell me."

"The only way to flush out the person or persons responsible is to put someone undercover in your office."

The alcohol hit hard on his empty stomach. He hadn't touched his meal. Thomas's eyebrow arched. Had he heard Rick correctly? "You want to run a covert op in my office?"

Rick's head bounced up and down like a bobblehead doll. "You told me you were in need of more staff. Right? This plan presents the perfect opportunity to slide one or more of our agents into place at your main office without causing suspicion."

Thomas rose, but grabbed for the edge of the table. Unsteady on his feet, he weaved and lurched forward. He felt Rick's arm slide around his waist to secure him from falling over. "And *who* do you think is qualified to do *that*, Einstein?"

A deep sultry, feminine voice rang out from the doorway. "I am, Thomas Hallock!"

All four men's heads turned, taking in the tall, stunning woman with sleek, jet-black hair hanging to her waist. She stood with her arms crossed, a look of pure disgust on her face as she took in the scene before her. Standing five-foot-ten inches tall, dressed in a dark brown leather bomber jacket and a white shirt tucked into her hip hugging jeans, the woman wore a police badge on her belt. Her smoky black eyes landed directly on her target – him.

She slowly approached the group, stopping just short of the table. Thomas tried to focus his eyes on the room's newest guest. In his semi-drunken state, the dawn of recognition hit him hard in the solar plexus when his eyes locked onto her familiar face.

He struggled to say anything remotely coherent. Finally, he exclaimed, "No way!" Glancing over at Rick, his eyebrows arched, and his eyes widened in surprise. His head whipped back around to take her in once more.

"*Squirt?* Is that really you?" Thomas stuttered, stunned.

From the look on her face, Thomas thought she'd been contemplating taking him out on the spot. She had every right to, given their past.

To everyone's horror, including that of the newest arrival, Thomas Hallock keeled over, face-first into the table, down for the count.

CHAPTER SIX

Courtney Stockton's life had been turned upside-down. No matter how the Director and Agent Tanner had framed the parameters of what she'd be accomplishing for the Hallock family and Rick's company, she could not stuff the past into the recesses of her mind. She thought she'd made a pretty wise career choice. One that would allow her to avoid Thomas since the night of Rick's thirtieth birthday party. In her adult version of "hide and seek," Courtney had successfully worked as a legitimate CIA operative during the last eleven years. That was until now. The hard work to maintain her distance from the man came crashing to an end last night when she'd been forced to face him. Well, in reality, Tom faced the table— literally—but his expression upon recognizing her would be forever embedded in her memory.

Her present predicament was not covered in the Agency manual. Down the hall, lying face first in *her* queen-sized, four-poster bed, on top of *her* new feather pillows and comforter, was the man himself. To top it off, he was snoring so loudly, the pages of her *Woman's Fitness* magazine, sitting on the nightstand, rippled in the breeze. She detested the "booze snore."

"Achoo!" Courtney clapped a hand over her mouth in an attempt to stifle a series of sneezes as well as sounds of the yawns that followed. Thomas's presence in her tiny apartment, coupled with his snoring, kept her awake most of the night. She was running on seventy-two hours of catnaps, and desperately in need of a severe jolt of caffeine.

As she sat on the closed lid of the toilet, she placed her head in her hands and groaned. For the thousandth time in the last twelve hours, she questioned the logic of why Thomas was not with her brother. His being in her apartment was *not* part of her job description.

Courtney stood and took a look into the oval bathroom mirror, trying to assess the damage of her sleepless night. She wasn't prepared for the image of the woman staring back. Good grief! She not only felt like hell, but the mirror confirmed she looked like a walking zombie. Dark circles, puffy, red eyes, all the remnants of a rough night. Readying herself for her daily jog, she pulled back her jet-black hair and wound it up into a ponytail using a thick rubber band. She rolled her head around in a circle in an attempt to relieve the kinks in her neck from sleeping on the tiny cramped loveseat in the apartment's living room.

Courtney hadn't been forced to sleep on a couch in quite a while. Her undercover digs at the villa in Positano, Italy were rather luxurious. With a cook, chauffeur, five bedrooms and seven bathrooms, and two hundred and sixty-five steps to her own private beach at her disposal, she'd had no reason to complain. After the grimy daily dealings with the art underworld, she came home to grandeur every night. Unfortunately, Salvatore came with the job and the villa. But with enough wine, mixed with a small sedative served at the late dinners, the older man didn't pose a problem. Now, she'd come one hundred and eighty degrees in her temporary living arrangements.

Slapping her cheeks, Courtney, tired and weary, snapped herself into a more proper frame of mind for her run. As a reward for completing her morning exercise routine, she was looking forward to getting a double mocha latte. The run was not the only thing on her agenda. If she didn't get a move on, she would be late for an important appointment. Yanking her running pants off the hook on the back of the bathroom door, she drew them on and pulled an old gray training tee shirt over her head.

Courtney slowly opened the bathroom door, praying it wouldn't creak. She snuck a peek down the hallway. Thomas's irritating snore still echoed from behind the closed bedroom door across the hall. Feeling like a burglar in her own home, she tiptoed to the apartment's newly remodeled kitchen. She used the kitchen counter to balance herself while she pulled on her sneakers.

Unplugging her iPhone from its charger, she scrolled down to her favorite playlist and clipped the phone to her pants. After slipping into a ratty sweatshirt, Courtney grabbed her keys and wallet from the table by the door. She let herself out of the apartment, double-checking that the door was locked. Joe would be up to wake Thomas soon enough. Knowing that, she made for the park across the street.

As her feet pounded the pavement, the music playing in her ears didn't help tune out her jumbled thoughts. Her mind wandered to a place she didn't want to go. A time and a place she'd tried so hard to avoid thinking about. She'd done a great job, or thought she had. Until now.

Normally, Courtney did her best thinking and strategizing on her feet. But it wasn't every day the man of one's dreams fell literally at one's feet. Courtney's had done so last night in fine fashion, face-first onto the pub table, leaving everyone around him, herself included, speechless and gasping out loud before rushing to his aid.

She couldn't help but flash back twenty years to the day she developed a bad case of puppy love for Thomas Hallock. She'd answered the door of the Stockton home in Hampton Beach, her pigtails dangling askew on each side of her head. Looking up, her heart flip-flopped at the sight of the man asking to see her brother. From that moment forward, Thomas weaseled his way into the special place deep within her heart with everything he did. Summer after summer, she often trailed Rick and his best friend whenever they allowed her to.

During her teen years, her biggest fear was he'd put two and two together and figure out she'd developed a full blown crush. She'd have been mortified had he one ounce of suspicion. There was no way her "townie" feelings could be reciprocated by the handsome, eligible Hampton socialite. It was foolish to even think she had a chance at a relationship, considering their age differences. Who would think he'd be remotely interested in her? But a girl could dream, couldn't she?

On the night of Rick's thirtieth birthday bash everything changed. Courtney turned twenty-one three weeks earlier. Downing one too many Jell-O shots, mixed with six cosmos, was the primary reason she woke up the next morning naked. And next to her lay Thomas's warm body spooned to hers. The night was somewhat of a blur. But she recalled the sex had been mind-blowing. Better than anything she'd imagined in her fantasies. Thomas had reached for her often through the night. Each time, Courtney let the love she felt for him shine through.

But morning came and Thomas awoke. The shock and embarrassment on his face sucker-punched her in the stomach. He'd snatched up the rumpled sheet and wrapped his naked torso, bolting from the bed they'd shared. He apologized over and over for taking advantage of her. Courtney tried to tell him how wrong he was. She wanted him to know it hadn't been a mistake. She loved him, and always had. But the man wouldn't listen.

Defeated, it finally registered he would never want to hear what she had to say. The feeling of his rejection tore through her gut. Deeply mortified, Courtney hightailed it out of his cottage, running barefoot down the drive to her car, her red-sequined ball gown barely zipped, her shoes in her hand.

Courtney fled Hampton Beach the very next day, at first making her way to friends in Washington, DC. She made up every excuse in the book to not return, and her family was devastated by her decision.

Then came the offer of a lifetime and an answer to her prayers. Trained like her brother with degrees in forensic accounting as well as art history from Georgetown University, she was sought out by Director Hallock to join the CIA. After graduating at the top of her class from the Farm, as they called their training facility, she volunteered for any mission that would put an ocean between her and Thomas. Over the years, she'd come to the conclusion he was the primary reason for her failed relationships. The men she'd attempted to date never measured up – to him. Thomas had set the bar too damn high.

When the call came from Sam Tanner, Courtney's stress level skyrocketed. Memories of that passionate night in Thomas's bed flooded her mind and haunted her on the flight from Rome. She and Thomas were once again on the same continent. Together. Things had come full circle. This time, the man was in *her* bed.

Courtney stopped short in her tracks. She was breathing hard and checked her pulse. Just as she suspected, her rate was on overload. She inhaled and exhaled and moved on, this time deciding to power walk instead.

Clear your head! Focus. Keep your eye on the objective of your mission. Be quick, do your job and get the hell out of Dodge.

As she walked to her destination, she glanced at her surroundings, the architecture of the brownstones and old buildings turned into loft apartments. Cars and trucks stuck in city traffic blared their horns. Cabs weaved in and out as they picked up passengers trying to flag them down.

Realizing she was wasting precious time, she found a bench in the park to cool off. She sat down and turned off her music, pulling out her ear buds. She wiped the sweat from her brow with the towel draped around her neck. Around her, couples and families played and laughed, enjoying what life had to offer. A normal life. Kids and families always tugged at her heartstrings. Times like these reminded her of what she often wished for: a life with Thomas, complete with a family to call her own.

What's wrong with you? When have you not been able to set aside personal biases to work professionally? Think about what Sam told you to do.

Aggravated as she was to have been withdrawn from her CIA mission before she'd made her collar and closed the deal, Courtney had to obey the Director's order. Add to that her brother's need of her expertise. When Thomas had solicited Rick's help, Courtney knew immediately Rick had reached out to Elizabeth Hallock. The scope of the operation was immense.

Courtney, whether she liked it or not, was making her return to Hampton Beach. Thomas Hallock had her made run. Now back, armed with a gun and a badge, she couldn't help but think life still sucked.

CHAPTER SEVEN

The Expresso Café

"Janie's dead." The somber voice came through the earpiece of Rick's phone.

Rick could barely contain his disbelief when Jim Benjamin, the Southampton Town Chief of Police, relayed the news.

His stomach plummeted. "You made a positive ID?"

"It didn't take long, what with the evidence."

"What happened?"

"Don't know. A couple taking their boat out early this morning from Long Wharf Pier thought a trash bag was snagged around the buoy. When they got closer they realized it was a body and dialed 911."

Rick almost lost his grip on his cell as he shook his head. "Listen, when the ME's office gets done with the autopsy and knows the TOD, text or call me back. This changes our plans."

He listened as Jim sounded off in his ear about the ongoing investigation. Not believing the new development, Rick shot back in a low voice, "Somebody got wind of her being undercover. When was the last time she checked in?"

"Three days ago," came the reply.

"*Three?* And you didn't think anything was up?" Rick was irate. "Hell. She was supposed to make inquiries discreetly, if she could. Weren't you worried? Hell, I would have been. Three days without a call would have had me combing the streets looking for her."

Jim didn't respond as quickly as he had before, which allowed time for Rick to take a swallow of his coffee. Now nervous and on edge from the news, he tried to remain calm by drumming his fingers on the wooden table of the booth he'd commandeered for his meeting.

He didn't want to tell Jim how to do his job, but he asked, "Are you going to pull Sammy in, to be safe? I'd call Geoff Daniels. He'd be more than willing to help you. His security detail from the farm could put the kid up in a safe house."

Considering the text Janie sent him three days before, it seemed the safest thing to suggest. Full of suspicion and mind reeling from the news, Rick thought it too coincidental Janie's texts stopped that morning. "Yeah. Listen, I got to go. I've got a meeting. We should be out there in a few days. Stay in touch."

Rick ended the call and pulled up what Janie sent him, reading through the texted information line by line. Anger and a strong sense of guilt welled up inside him. He really should have shared Janie's suspicions with Jim right then, but until he had a better understanding of what happened to her, he felt he couldn't trust anybody outside his team's circle. Rick placed the phone on vibrate mode and clipped it to his belt.

Janie Walker was dead! Rick was good at profiling people. Something didn't gel. Janie was street smart. Given what they'd asked her to do, he knew she'd have taken extreme measures to be careful.

She'd been a troubled soul as a teenager, a high school dropout, but she was smart enough and savvy enough to work the judicial system. Her pro bono attorney convinced Jim to let her work odd jobs for the STPD to satisfy a plea deal with the District Attorney. She'd been feeding the department important tidbits of the darker side of what occurred beyond the dunes in the Hamptons for months. She had the unique knack, given her looks, to transform her appearance in order to travel in circles from the seedy to the upscale side of the Hamptons.

It was more imperative than ever he take a step back and rethink how to get Courtney inside the Hallock farm's office without anyone becoming suspicious of her sudden reappearance. He'd have to start wracking his brain for a Plan B and C.

Before Janie and Sammy were released to do their work in their "community service," Jim assured Rick he had handpicked the officers for the task force to be used in Thomas's case. With a sudden chill running down his spine, he knew he'd have to use and hide his own resources wisely. Everyone had to have a credible role – even family members. Which brought up an important question. Had Janie's backup dropped the ball, or did she somehow give her bodyguards the slip for some unknown reason?

Rick looked at the clock on the wall. Courtney was late. She more than likely had run up and down the path in the park an extra ten times to temper her frustration. Sitting in a window booth of the Expresso Café, he looked out over the busy street, his eyes alert for signs of any unusual behavior in the crowds milling about on the sidewalk outside.

Hearing the jingling of a bell located above the coffee shop's door, Rick turned to see his sister make her appearance. Courtney made her way to the serving counter and placed her order.

Rick attempted to get her attention. "Court! Over here!"

She turned, looked over her shoulder and acknowledged his

presence with a scowl. As he waited for her to come and sit down, his mind was awhirl with all the current information he had to relay. By the glare she'd sent his way, it was evident she hadn't forgiven him for last night. Rick knew he placed her in an awkward position, but there'd been no other choice. When Thomas passed out, there was only one place to take him — the safehouse, three flights up above the Red Lion, which just happened to be her temporary living quarters.

To make matters simple, the Director worked out a deal with Joe to have Courtney rent the apartment, leaving a legitimate paper trail in case someone might question her return to the States. Giving her a cover as a CPA working for an international firm with an office in New York City had, before all this, been a perfect fit. Was it still going to work? Going to the Hamptons was going to pose the biggest problem.

A few years ago, Courtney bought back the old family homestead in Hampton Beach. Working with a top-notch architect, she completely redesigned the house from top to bottom. Throughout their lives, she'd surprised him. He was truly proud of her accomplishments and, above all, when she'd stepped up to save the family when their mother passed away. Not the eldest, she nurtured his brothers and sisters, as well as himself and their alcoholic father. As young as she was, Court worked two, sometimes three jobs during the summer months, helping make ends meet. Her buying back the family homestead opened up a whole new world for the Stockton clan. They were no longer seen as "townies." The house was a showcase, like many of the older estate houses, but with a truly homey feel for all who stepped through its door. Family meant everything to Courtney. The door of the family home was open to everyone, even though she herself chose to live a solitary life with the CIA elsewhere.

Coming at him like a lioness ready to pounce on her prey,

Rick sat up straight. He had to keep his guard up. Courtney had a way of winning an argument before he even knew he'd surrendered.

Sliding into the other side of the booth, Courtney undid the lid of her large mocha latte. She sat in stony silence for the first few minutes, sipping the hot drink. Her smoky black eyes scanned the crowd, then steadied her attention on him. From his experience, her dagger-like glare meant one of two things. One, Court was plotting her next move, which he wouldn't like. Or, two, she might unleash her tempered fury without a thought to who was sitting around them. Rick had his money on the latter.

Here she blows. Rick let go of his cup and leaned against the cushioned back of the booth putting distance between them for extra protection.

"Good morning...*traitor.* Did *you* sleep well?" Court enunciated her last four words.

It was a loaded question. Rick carefully contemplated his reply. "Yup. Like a baby."

Suddenly, Courtney grabbed him by the strings of the hood of his sweatshirt and yanked his body halfway across the table until he came nose to nose with her.

"Well, I sure as hell didn't!" Her voice was a hushed whisper, clear and distinct.

No doubt about it. Court was pissed. He'd bet his paycheck something had gone down at the apartment after he and Joe left her with Thomas. She wasn't pleased then, and she *certainly* wasn't a happy camper now. But being her brother, he couldn't help but relish provoking her just a tiny bit. He placed his hands on hers, freeing himself and his sweatshirt from her grasp.

"Whoa! Whoa! Whoa! Something got your dander up? You look pissed...sis." Rick made himself comfortable, giving thanks his coffee hadn't spilled in her fit of anger. Glancing down, he spied the nearly empty cup. He looked over his shoulder at the line which now wound its way throughout the shop. Nope. No time for a refill. He and Courtney had too much to discuss. His java jolt would have to wait. It was imperative he tell her the change in plans, especially given the news of Janie Walker's death.

Rick eyed her cautiously as she sat with her arms crossed over her chest, defiant.

"Don't give me that doe-eyed, innocent look, Rick. Thomas Hallock is sleeping in *my* apartment! Explain, why, in the dead of night, you couldn't have thrown him in the back of a cab and taken him to *your* penthouse? Why did he have to end up with me?"

"He had unexpected company at the St. Regis."

"What?" Courtney's voice rose. "Somebody followed him?" She paused, tapping her fingers on the table. "Damn, I had a feeling that would happen."

"Lower your voice." Rick pressed his fingers to his lips.

Courtney leaned across the table. "Three days ago, I get a call from Sam to get my butt back to DC, only to land and be whisked off to New York City. I'm going over the documents he gave me in the briefing when I get a text from Joe telling me to come downstairs ASAP. Imagine my surprise to discover *you* need *me* to get Thomas under control." His sister paused, pointing her finger in his face. "It was my understanding I'd come on board this case when there was enough probable cause established to work the overseas angle." Her voice drifted off, but Rick knew she wasn't finished ranting. "You know perfectly well this is going to get complicated."

Rick put up his hands. "Look. It's like I said. I followed two men into the bar where I met Thomas. They'd parked themselves at a nearby table. One was a tall, older man, big, hair graying at his temples. The other, I'd say, was in his late twenties. Court, there was something about the second guy that looked familiar. I can't, for the life of me, put my finger on where I've seen him, but I know I have. I subtly managed to grab a photo of the duo using the bar's mirror. It's not the greatest quality, but I sent it off to my contact in the Hampton Beach PD. I hope he'll be able to identify who it is. I realized there wasn't much time to get Tom safely to Joe's."

"Is that what the Director wanted?"

"Yeah, she made that call. So before you go ballistic again, that's the reason we had to move Tom up into your digs." Rick raised his hand to ward off her retort. "Had we any other option, I'd have taken him to my place.

"On our way to Joe's, I called the Director. She made it perfectly clear, from that point on, Joe would be our interim contact to the Agency. I don't need to reiterate she wants everything on the QT, considering the family angle."

Courtney shook her head in disbelief. "I can't believe her family's in another precarious situation."

"I know. Me, either. But getting back to Tom. We originally planned for you to use your expertise in forensic accounting to handle whatever was needed on the international financial front. We still do."

"And the Director's approved this?" Rick was surprised by the look of disbelief on his sister's face. He couldn't believe her reaction, considering her briefing with Sam Tanner on her way to the Big Apple. He could have sworn she knew what she was in for.

"Given the people involved, she has no choice. When the magnitude of the embezzlement scam came to fruition yesterday, we realized the entire infrastructure of the farm's finances were compromised. We're going to have to use some of the Director's resources after what my two IT guys uncovered."

"This is déjà vu." Courtney cracked her knuckles. "The third time in a little over three years her family's gone through major money crises."

"Copy that. My team confirmed this is in no way related to what Mr. Hallock was involved in three years ago. But I'm getting off-track." He reached across the table and took his sister's hand. "Court, I don't need to tell *you*, of all people, things don't always go according to plan. You know what needs to be done. You're the trained operative."

"With Thomas hanging out at my place how am I supposed to do my job? I can't babysit him 24/7. I've got my own ops to plan and conduct."

If anything, Courtney was persistent when it came to the topic of Thomas. He playfully wiggled his eyebrows to break the tension, but she glared at him. Without warning, she suddenly reached over the table and popped him in the right shoulder, the one he'd just had rehabbed from rotator cuff surgery.

"Ouch. That hurt!" What had her so riled up? It was if she had an axe to grind.

"I feel like Goldilocks. Someone's sleeping in my bed, and it sure as hell isn't me!"

Rick had never worked a case with his sister. They were both Type A personalities. Egos were going to clash. He had to make it clear to her he was the one calling the shots. She was going to have to answer to him for the time being.

Rick leaned back, his arms across his chest. He leveled a pointed look at his sister's haggard expression. "What's going on, Court? I've never seen you this agitated. Tom's staying. I could kick myself that we hadn't thought to be more cautious, especially given the phone call I just got from the Southampton Police."

"What call? What's going on?" With that one piece of information dangling as a carrot in front of her nose, Rick had her full attention.

"Jim Benjamin and I sent Janie Walker, a trusted informant, out into the community to see what she might be able to pick up. We had her check into whether or not new people had settled in town. Perhaps somebody might seem out of place. Typical stuff. We thought she'd be able to get a whiff of 'townie' talk."

"And? How does this relate to the call?"

"Early this morning, a couple leaving a marina in Sag Harbor saw something bobbing in the water. The man took out his drag hook and snagged what he thought was a huge garbage bag. Unfortunately, at the other end of that hook was Janie." He paused upon seeing the stunned expression on his sister's face. "Jim says it looks like an amateur job. Whoever was responsible didn't realize the tide schedule. My take is someone needed to dump her in a hurry."

"So what's happening out there now?"

"Jim's beefing up security around Hallock Farm and the family. That includes Tom's Southampton office, house and the apartment he uses from time to time when he doesn't want to ramble alone in that huge beach home. As for you and my team, I think we need a few more days to strategize where and how to set up a base of operations. It can't be detected. Then, using the intel, we can set up the sting. It would be wise if you, the Director and I had a final meeting before we head out."

"What about Joe?"

"Joe's got his marching orders. His contacts have been activated. My men will utilize them at some point."

Courtney crushed her Styrofoam cup into a ball, placing it on the table. Her hands trembled. "Well, this certainly puts a different spin on things, doesn't it?"

The hitch in her reply had Rick thinking she was juggling something emotionally. A professional job brought her home by orders from Director Hallock. But what else could have her reacting so out of character?

She stared him down once again. "Have you given any thought as to the explanation you're going to give Thomas as to why I'm back? I evaded him for eleven years, and last night I burst in, looking to take the man down. He saw my badge on my belt. I'm sure of it, Rick. How about I just blurt out, 'Oh! By the way, I've been undercover with the CIA!'"

"Get serious, Court." Rick wanted to move on. "Listen to yourself. You're sounding completely irrational – and unprofessional."

"Well, I'll just tell him the truth, then. 'I fell in love with you, and since the feelings weren't mutual, I ran away. Oh and while we're on the subject, you ruined me for every decent man I ever tried to get close to.' Sounds like a soppy romance novel, doesn't it?" Courtney dropped the cup she'd been playing with. Her hand shot up and covered her mouth. Too late.

Rick sat stunned, not knowing how to react to what Courtney had dropped in his lap. *I knew there'd been something to drive her away! She valued our family too much to run.*

How should he respond? Courtney had never, *ever* shared her personal life. He had to admit there were times he thought maybe something had transpired between his best friend and his sister, but he'd always dismissed the thought. Tom would have said something. One look at his sister told him she was trying desperately to mask the pain she still felt.

Then it dawned on him. "If it's the night I'm thinking of, you're not twenty-one anymore. Give yourself some credit." He held up his hand, cutting off any response she tried to make. "I don't want details. Whatever happened is in the past. It's *over*."

Courtney turned and gazed out the shop's window. He watched as she struggled to hold back tears. He wouldn't have believed it unless he'd seen it with his own eyes. His hard core, CIA operative sister still must have feelings for his best friend! Now, things made sense – her demeanor, her attitude toward the case. She'd never forgotten, but most importantly, never forgiven Tom.

The objective of his investigation was to restore the Hallock fortunes and bring the perpetrators to justice. Given the call from Jim and the knowledge of Courtney's predicament, plans needed to be tweaked.

The sooner, the better.

CHAPTER EIGHT

Courtney wanted Rick to cut to the chase. She was back solely to do a job and bring closure to the mess at Hallock Farm. She wanted to get back to Positano ASAP to wrap up her mission there. She'd invested the last two years in Operation Roman Holiday. Courtney wanted that collar on *her* record. The Director had promised her a promotion if she succeeded.

"Earth to Rick!" She snapped her fingers to get her brother's attention. He had as much, if not more, on his mind now as she did. He, too, had to struggle with the battle of keeping his personal feelings from encroaching into his professional world.

"I'm sorry. What were you saying?" Rick asked.

"What's the plan to proceed with Tom? He'll want to nitpick every detail."

Rick pushed aside his empty coffee cup and leveled "the look." She braced herself for a dressing-down.

Rick's forefinger tapped the table to make his point. "First and foremost, Thomas is my client."

"So when is your *client*," she said through clenched teeth, "going elsewhere?"

Her brother's shoulders tensed. He combed his fingers

through his hair and tugged at his earlobe. Whenever Rick had something he really didn't want to share, he signaled, just as he'd done when they were kids. It was how they communicated around their old man.

"Court, I can't…we can't…" Rick usually thought quick on his feet, but with the newly discovered information that came to light last night, coupled with a dead body, the timetable to accomplish what needed to be done had to be completely reconfigured. "We've got no choice. For now, Tom's got to stay under guard. We can't let him out of our sight. He needs protection." Before Courtney could reply, Rick shot up his hand. "For the record, no more than two days."

Courtney kept the volume of her voice low. "No! He can't be underfoot. I've got work to do." She bit down on her lower lip, wondering how she was going to deal with her personal demons while maintaining her professional cool. In her previous cases with the CIA, she never encountered a dilemma where her emotions played into the job to get done. Sure, sometimes she had to get "close" to her subjects, but those people were nothing more to her than "paper-dolls." Her objectivity was never compromised. *This* case was going to be the challenge of a lifetime.

"I never brought up the subject of you and Tom, although it crossed my mind years ago. Always figured it was your business. If you wanted to talk to me, you would. Whatever 'it' was." Rick curled his fingers into quotation marks in the air. "I'm going to venture a guess, considering your reaction, that 'it' was a painful experience you'd like to forget." Rick paused. "From here on out, you've got to stuff those emotions in a box and be rational. No dramatics. You know we can't move him. Not with somebody watching. A van was spotted across the street from my condo last night. It's no secret Tom and I go way back. I'm praying we can keep what's going on under wraps, but if not, people will definitely surmise I'd be the first person he would turn to for help. The Hampton Beach PD is involved, as well as Jim's squad. The Director is making sure there's money for extra man-power."

"So how are you going to fit me in, since I'm entering into this operation earlier than planned?"

"You'll go undercover at Tom's Southampton office. We'll slide you in to work with Jack Jessup, the new CEO Tom hired. You can live in your house in Hampton Beach. It's a short commute. Besides, the house is going to be the base of operations."

If Courtney didn't know how smart and respected her brother was, she'd swear he had rocks for brains. Was he kidding? He really thought that after rebuilding the family home and supposedly being away at some cushy job with an internationally based accounting firm, she was just going to waltz back into town to take a demotion in the eyes of the corporate world? In the Hamptons? She shook her head and eyed her brother reflectively. "*Not* going to work."

"What do you mean? The Director's already signed off. You're coming home to go to work for the Hallocks because Thomas will be taking a break as the CFO. You're going to step in. If anyone asks, you tell them you decided you had enough of London. You wanted to be closer to home and family. It's the perfect cover. Anthony and Troy don't think it will take long to flush out the embezzlers. We can't go changing things."

"Look, Einstein. Everyone who's lived in town for years knows who I am. People will question every move I make, especially since I left in such a damn hurry. My leaving was fodder for the morning breakfast club at Eckart's for months. How's it going to look for me to go working *for* Hallock Farm? People know my background, where I've supposedly been, and how high up the corporate ladder I've gone. The wrong people will put two and two together easily. You just said you want to use our house as base camp. That'll work, but Andrew and Troy tramping in and out will raise eyebrows. You need to justify their cover. It's going to be hard in those two small towns to be new *and* keep a low profile. I hate to burst your bubble, but your idea is simply not going to pan out. Too many holes."

Touché. Courtney sat back in the booth and leveled an "I told you so look" across the table.

Then it dawned on her. The solution had nothing to do with the fact she was a CIA agent with one of the highest intelligence clearances or a background in forensic accounting. Courtney had worked some of the most difficult international crime scams. Her knowledge of mathematical jargon and logic solved any case she'd been presented by using real world mathematical modeling. Her algorithms were never wrong. She excelled in cryptology. In addition, her knowledge of economic policies and procedures that existed inside and outside the US borders landed her private invitations to the Oval Office of several administrations. She was a genius at making something out of nothing, as evidenced by her bank accounts.

"I don't like that smug look on your face, Courtney Ellen," Rick said. "You've got something up your sleeve. And it's *not* on the Director's agenda."

Courtney smiled slyly. She wasn't sure whether or not he'd be mad or shocked. But she had to make him see reason. Her idea would prove worthy, and most of all, believable. Her "Plan B" was the *only* way out of the dilemma everybody faced upon their return to Hampton Beach: Thomas, Rick, Rick's team and herself. "I've got a different take on this…" She waved her hand. "It's perfectly foolproof."

She was so pleased with what she was about to tell him she beamed and practically purred with delight.

Rick squirmed in his seat.

She loved being the one in control. "*If* Thomas will go along with *my* idea, we'll be able to get to Hampton Beach sooner rather than later."

Rick eyed her warily, sounding leery. "I can't make any promises until I hear what cards you lay on the table."

"Then I'm out of here if you won't hear me out. You can be the one to tell the Director all bets are off. I'll head back across the pond tonight."

"You can't."

"Why not?"

"You'd be brought up on insubordination charges." The man sat back, looking very pleased with himself.

Disgusted, Courtney didn't have time for games. There was an unwanted man in her bed. If Thomas was awake, he could possibly be rummaging through her neatly ordered closet. Her *private* world. He might find her secret box — the one with all the pictures taken of him over the years and the letters he'd written her when she attended Georgetown. The box even had the shells he'd found along the beach and given her as "presents" when she'd been little. She had to get back. Her heart raced as she started to panic, thinking of what he might be doing to entertain himself if Joe wasn't around.

Rick grabbed her chin and forced her to look at him. He was clearly frustrated. "We're out of time. Make your point."

"Thomas and I are going to get engaged. Operation Bride and Groom is about to commence."

With that brief statement, Courtney slid out of the bench and made her way out of the coffee shop, hoping her brother was trying to pry his jaw off the table.

CHAPTER NINE

Main Beach Club
East Hampton

Jason Rockwell sat in the back of the black Town Car, its engine idling. He'd made his driver hide the large car behind a copse of scrub pines off to the side of the main parking lot. He wanted the engine running in case they had to make a hasty retreat. It wasn't Jason's choice to meet at Main Beach, but the man soon to make his appearance had insisted. The area was usually unoccupied at this time of year. There was a harsh chill in the air, not a good day for beach walkers or surfers. The Town Car, at present, was the only car in the massive parking lot.

"There's a car coming, boss." Mark, his driver and bodyguard, pointed out the front windshield to an approaching dark SUV.

"Keep your eye on your mirror. If the car pulls up to the pilings by the beach and taps the brakes twice, it's him. He knows where to find me," Jason responded.

As Jason waited, he prayed no one lurked about. It was a dark, gloomy day. Sleet and rain had been predicted, keeping people away from the only public access to the ocean in the area. In the summertime, the sun would shine brightly, giving a glare off the ocean. Beach dwellers would vie for parking spaces and unload their gear for a long day of romping in the surf and soaking up the sun.

At this time of year, the trek out to the Hamptons hadn't begun in full force, which worked to Jason's advantage. Houses, stores and streets were empty except for the locals. But the locals could be detrimental to his operations, as he'd discovered several times. Lately, he'd had to be careful where he conducted his business and with whom.

His driver checked the mirrors. "It's him, boss."

A few minutes later, someone knocked on the rear door's window. *Tap-tap….* Silence…*Tap-tap.*

"Unlock the door," Jason ordered as he reached into his coat pocket, wrapping his hand around the handle of a small pistol, his finger on the trigger. "Put up the privacy screen. If I rap, get us the hell out of here."

The lock released, and the back door of the Town Car opened. A large, burly man, dressed in a black leather coat and black pants, slid in beside him. He wore a dark skullcap on his head and took up the majority of the remaining back seat. Jason wasn't used to seeing the man sans uniform, but was grateful he had the foresight to dress down in case he'd run into anyone in town. It would appear as if he had the day off.

"You're late," Jason growled. "Let me get straight to the point. I've got a dead body on my hands. You care to explain that? You told me you had this worked out."

"About that - " the deep masculine voice replied, only to be cut off.

"Stop." Jason tried to temper the anger surging within him over the last several hours as he stewed about the situation. "Did the girl get too close to my operation?"

"Yes. I found out through the local grapevine she asked

some pointed questions, especially when she was waitressing at that restaurant. Then, she started hanging around the café by Hallock's office. I know for a fact she overheard a conversation she shouldn't have."

"So you took care of things?"

"I think so."

"I don't want you to think, I want you to know!" Jason roared. "We're too far in for any stupid mistakes leading back to you or me. Are you positive she didn't pass on tidbits of what she gleaned to anyone else? What about that kid she's been hanging around with?"

"Positive. It's taken care of. Let it go."

Looking at the man sitting next to him, Jason could see a steely glare in his eyes. Obviously, the authority figure didn't like being second-guessed.

Time to change the subject. "What's the status on that thumb drive?"

"Gone." The man's jaw clenched tight.

"Gone? What do you mean gone? I thought Hailey was supposed to pass it off to you. We needed those invoices that were loaded onto it." Jason's heart raced.

"Hailey told me she typed in the data and was about to close the office when Hallock showed up out of the blue. Said he never comes into the office at that time of day. He asked for the thumb drive, so she had no recourse but to give it to him. He informed her he had a meeting that wasn't on his calendar. Then he abruptly left."

"She didn't have time to back up the new set of files?"

The man pounded his fist into the door. "No. I'm not too happy about that, either. But she's resourceful. Don't worry. I trust her to figure out a way to hack into what she's working on. She'll get us what's needed."

Releasing his grip on the gun in his pocket, Jason rubbed

his hands over his face to stem some of his frustration. Trying to sound calm, he asked, "Why did I ever think I could put her in that office? She can't do what we need done. But damn! Hailey should have known better. She's got the IT background to stay one step ahead of everyone due to all those degrees she earned. How she could have slipped up?" It was his turn to slam his hand against the armrest.

"No offense, Jason, but Hailey's new to this kind of activity. Give her a break."

Jason was exasperated with the turn of events. He'd never wanted to use Hailey like this. She was his sister. She knew all about the kinds of businesses he'd transacted in his sordid past. A few legit, most not.

Hailey adored him, no matter what his particular pedigree. Jason raised her, with the help of nannies, after their parents were killed. Ten years older, Jason saw Hailey attended the best schools on the inheritance money left in the family's trust. When it came to doing for Hailey, anything he spent on her came from his legitimate company dividends. He'd wanted no questions asked regarding anything "irregular" in her background. The girl had made him proud. He marveled at the woman she'd become: driven, headstrong, graduating number one in her class at MIT. The only thing they'd ever truly disagreed on was her taking a year abroad after college "to see the world." No bodyguards. Just a good pair of walking shoes and a backpack...and one very close friend whom he had vetted and approved of.

Hailey understood Jason too well, as far as he was concerned. She knew he was desperate to get back at Thomas. Although she'd been a child, his actions as a teenager had negatively affected her, as well. Totally turned off by the demands of the high school classroom and not making the football team, Jason had allowed his grades to falter. When his parents discovered how close he was to flunking out and why, they threatened to ship him off to live with his aunt and uncle if he didn't straighten up and fly right. Not only did he ignore them, he became even more rebellious. One night, at one of the local beach parties that were so prevalent with the townies in those days, Jason plied fifteen-year-old Shari Dowling with booze, in the hope of scoring a little action from the pretty teen. Enter the white knights of the Hamptons, Tom Hallock and Rick Stockton. Outraged, they stepped in before anything nefarious happened. Thomas not only took the girl home, he told her parents what had almost occurred. The Dowlings, in turn, confronted the Rockwells with their son's behavior. Jason found himself shipped off to his aunt and uncle in Queens, never to return until after his parents' death.

Uncle Walter owned an import/export business, a legit company until Jason, ambitious and thirsting for vengeance, started doing some side work with a group of Russian mobsters. Decades had passed while Jason amassed his fortune and waited, dreaming of the day he could return to the Hamptons and destroy Thomas Hallock's life, strip him of everything he knew and loved, leaving him alone and abandoned, just as Jason himself had been.

Then, one day, Hailey approached him with the perfect plan. While on a nationwide job search site, she'd seen the advertisement for an IT/CPA to head the accounting department at the Hallock farm's main office in Southampton. She jumped at the chance to work for Tom's company as her first job out of college. Her announcement she was pursuing the job to help him extract his revenge floored him.

He had adamantly said no at first. He pleaded with her to have the life he'd always sought, the recognition and wealth she deserved, a life that was legal and aboveboard. Hailey rebutted with a firm, "I'm going to apply." After much soul searching on his part, he acquiesced and told her to "go for it" – with parameters. She had set up interviews with the chain of command and was questioned by the board of directors. Hailey informed him that Elizabeth Hallock, in fact, voiced her strong disapproval of Jason's business practices. Still, Hailey must have played her role well, as she was offered the job on a six-month trial basis.

Now the perfect conduit to Thomas's movements in and out of the office, she'd been given the task of monitoring the new installation of the updated computer system to improve efficiency within the business. Being in control, she told him, allowed her to incorporate viruses into the system at a later date. It was then her brother could do what he and his partner wanted done – primarily gain access to the funds of the farm and deplete Thomas into bankruptcy. Already the hacking had begun, and monies had been diverted to Switzerland and off-shore accounts.

The man beside him cleared his throat, bringing Jason back to the here and now. He wrung his hands and eyed the man staring stonily at him. His visitor was making him nervous. Jason hated to admit it, but he needed the man's expertise and ability to get on the inside of the STPD. However, unlike his sister, this guy was dispensable should the occasion arise. Jason hoped it wouldn't come to that.

"Jason!" A gruff voice snapped at him. He turned his attention back to his companion. "*You* better think of a strategy to get that money transferred faster. Hallock hired Stockton to investigate the disappearing money trail. Word has it Rick's been on the case for a little over a week."

"Stockton? That means his IT team is already trying to hack their way into Hailey's encrypted system." Of course, Thomas would turn to his best friend, especially with a case of this magnitude.

"It's a good thing your sister's got a reputation for being one of the number one programmers in the country. You have to warn her, JR. Call her tonight. Better yet, let me give her a ring."

Jason saw a semblance of a smile forming at the corners of his visitor's mouth.

What I wouldn't give to slap his face. Smug, arrogant bastard. One for the dead body I hadn't planned on and two, for his attraction to my kid sister.

Hailey's take was that the man was simply a flirt. She'd reassured Jason it wasn't anything she couldn't handle. But Jason didn't want the man within three feet of her. Present circumstances made that too possible. Jason mentally made a note to teach his sister how to use his spare Glock.

For now, mindful of the time, he had several more questions for his companion. "Did you find out if Director Hallock's involved?"

Leaning back in the cushy, leather seat, he commented, "I've heard nothing regarding Elizabeth. But I've got feelers out. Right now, Rick is handling everything. What do you want me to do?"

"First, let's get back to the issue of Janie Walker."

"Like I told you. She got too deep, stuck her nose into issues that didn't concern her. She was overheard at Hampton Coffee asking one of the locals about Hailey. I forgot who told me Janie knew about the thumb drive."

Jason didn't believe the man. He was playing dumb, and it wasn't sitting well. "Who could possibly have told her? She was just a street junkie." Jason couldn't wrap his head around the fact that, in just a few days, Janie had managed to dig up key pieces of information. Had she been on to Hailey? His biggest concern was the fact she may have shared her findings with someone else. But who? If the guy next to him didn't know, then who would?

"My information came from a very reliable source, one I trust implicitly. Jason, killing Janie wasn't in the cards. Listen, I tried to reach you, but your assistant said you were out of the office. She wouldn't give me your contact number."

"I wasn't happy getting back and hearing the news this morning. Next time you find the need to do something drastic, you run it by me, no matter what. You got that? My people will know where I am. You know who they are. There was no reason you couldn't have contacted any one of them. Are we clear on that?"

A string of frustrated curses erupted from the man beside him. Jason prayed he'd at least been smart enough to have someone else carry out his dirty work.

He waited for a response, but none was forthcoming. "If you don't like the way we're going to play this, you can jump ship anytime." Because of their closeness, Jason felt every muscle in the man's body tense. "If you're not happy, spit it out. We can part company right now. I'll pay you what I owe you…. But understand the people I work for may not drop your involvement. There will be consequences, if you catch my drift."

Suddenly, Jason's driver rapped on the privacy panel. Jason hit the button to lower the window.

"What?"

"Someone's turned the corner about five blocks up. Could be a patrol car. It's moving pretty slow. We better get out of here, boss."

Jason turned to take in the man beside him. He'd aged a lot over the last several years. But, he'd wanted in when the original plans were designed to bring Hallock to his knees. Both men were tired of the Hallocks flaunting their power and their millions while the rest of them "got by." They lived well, but not in the way they truly wanted to indulge themselves. Both wanted the lifestyle Hallock had been privileged to live. Their goal was to take his money and run - build a new life outside of the States. Somewhere where there was no extradition treaty. First, though, Jason would see Thomas Hallock humbled — abandoned by his family, publicly shamed, and flat broke. Only then would the Rockwells' revenge be complete.

"Go!" Jason commanded, pushing the man toward the door. "Where'd you get that car? That's not your normal mode of transportation."

"I borrowed Corey's Jeep. Told him I was having car problems. Had to pick up my date for brunch."

For the first time, Jason laughed out loud. "That's a good one. I hope he believed you. You haven't had a date in awhile." *And if I have anything to say about it, you're not dating my sister in the near future, either.*

As the visitor opened the car's back door, he turned to look directly at Jason, eyes glaring. "I'll be in touch as soon as I have any more information."

"Use the burner phone."

"Like you don't think I don't know to do that?"

A cold blast of sea air blew into the car, making Jason shiver. A chill ran down his spine. The window rattled from the impact of the slamming of the car door as the man left. The meeting had him spooked. He shook off the feeling of dread. "Get us out of here. Now!"

As the Town Car rolled out from behind the pine trees, the driver asked, "Where to?"

"Home. I'm out way past curfew."

His driver chuckled. "That missus of yours, boss, is tougher than some of those men we've gone to meet. She should work for you."

As the car took off, Jason tried to relax, but found it

impossible to do so. It was even more imperative now he not let his guard down. Since Rick Stockton had been hired by Hallock to look into the affairs at the office, Jason was going to need some serious backup for Hailey. He pulled out his iPhone to place a call to his sister. She needed to be told immediately about Stockton's investigation. But what worried Jason the most, knowing Rick for more than twenty years, was the man's reputation. He was damn good at what he did. A veritable bulldog.

But, Jason was ready. Come hell or high water, he was going to see Thomas Hallock ruined.

CHAPTER TEN

Thomas slowly sat up in bed, turned and planted his feet firmly on the floor. That small amount of movement had him raising his hand to massage his right temple in an attempt to assuage the piercing pain. Memories of the previous evening were a blur. When he blinked, events flashed through his mind. It had been that final shot of Grey Goose, followed by the downing of the pint of Guinness that produced the whopper of a hangover. His mouth felt dry, parched. He'd definitely woken up in worse shape before, what with carousing the Hampton social scene, all part of his duty as CFO. Tying one on hadn't been in the cards when yesterday started.

He vaguely remembered being dragged up three flights of stairs after blacking out. Keeping his head as still as possible, he took in his surroundings. The bed was a mess, the sheets and comforter rolled up into a ball at the foot of the bed. Thomas figured he must have suffered a fretful night's sleep. No surprise, with the stress of the last two weeks. His clothes were thrown over a chaise in the corner of the small, stark room. So much for paying five thousand dollars for a Gucci suit only to toss it into a mangled mess. As he looked into the full-length mirror hanging on the closet door, he saw he'd been stripped of his clothes. He wore nothing but a pair of black Jockey briefs.

Then it all came rushing back. Squirt. Amend that. Courtney Stockton. She'd been dressed like a tigress in a bomber jacket, her eyes flashing. That sleek black mane of hair hung almost to her waist, and a police badge shone brightly on her belt. He vaguely recalled shouting out her name before succumbing to the darkness. His head must have come in contact with the table, judging by the small, painful bump he felt above his right eye. He remembered Rick and Joe saying something about a "safe house."

Was this Joe's apartment? Rubbing his eyes for clarity, he took another look about. There seemed little evidence of it belonging to the Red Lion's proprietor. Suddenly, his eyes spied the infamous bomber jacket draped over a chair near the bed, along with a pair of jeans and a white shirt. It was then he knew the identity of the apartment's owner. He hadn't been that far gone to forget the "uniform" she wore that emphasized every curve of her body.

As his vision became clearer, he spied the closet in front of him, its doors wide open. Thomas's brow furrowed upon seeing a series of blue suits lined up next to white blouses. Underneath, pairs of blue pumps were meticulously lined up one next to the other. Perplexed, he shook his head. Last night, Courtney wore the attire of a cop on the beat. Maybe, undercover. The clothes in the closet were not your typical street cop/detective attire. Those in front of him were more in keeping with the wardrobe of a field agent in the FBI.

An image appeared in his mind. One of a woman, a much *older* woman whom he loved dearly. She was dressed in a dark blue suit, crisp white shirt with blue pumps. Her trademark reading glasses sat perched atop her head.

No! Could it be possible? Had Aunt Elizabeth recruited Courtney to work for the CIA? Was that why she'd disappeared from the face of the earth all these years?

Swiveling to see what else lurked in the bedroom, his eyes locked on an antique dresser. Most women of his acquaintance would have at least ten bottles of perfume sitting atop the bureau, along with an extremely large jewelry box overflowing with necklaces and bracelets. The top of the dresser was barren, but it looked as if a bomb had exploded. Every drawer was opened. Bras, panties, tee shirts and running pants hung out of each of the four drawers. The owner had obviously left in a hurry.

Deciding he better make an attempt to get himself together before Rick or Joe appeared, Thomas struggled to stand. He immediately fell back onto the mattress as the room spun, but not before his eyes spied a small, decorated tin box, tucked in the bottom left hand corner of the closet.

Another flashback hit him – the memory of two giggling little girls sitting at the Stockton kitchen table putting together their "treasure boxes." If he remembered correctly, this particular box was Courtney's. He was tempted to open it and see its contents. Why was it here in this sparsely decorated room?

Thomas smiled, thinking of Courtney growing from pigtails and freckles into a beautiful woman. A woman he'd made love to over and over again as if his life depended on it one summer's night. Then he woke up and opened his big mouth, tripping over his tongue, saying all the wrong things. He knew the minute he'd put a sword through her heart. She turned and left him… gone. Until last night. Words couldn't describe the depth of her beauty now, all these years later. He began to grow hard, his mind conjuring up her nakedness and comparing it to the curvaceous beauty who'd bested him last night.

He heard the front door to the apartment open.

"Tom, are ye awake?" A deep Irish brogue echoed down the hallway.

"In the bedroom," he replied, wincing in pain. Better to face Joe than Rick at this juncture of the morning. As intoxicated as he'd been, he vaguely remembered the disgust in Rick's eyes as he was dumped into bed by his best friend.

A strong string of Irish curses could be heard as Joe walked down the hallway and approached the bedroom door. No doubt his aunt was already in possession of a report of his conduct from the previous evening. Thomas sat on the bed, his head in his hands. He prayed that Joe would take pity on him after last night's debacle.

* * *

Thomas watched the door close. Joe left shaking his head, no doubt perturbed by what he'd found when he'd arrived in the apartment. He'd taken one look at Thomas sitting in his rumpled state and dragged, as the man put it quite succinctly, "his sorry arse" into the bathroom.

"Undress!" Joe bellowed. The smaller man's Irish brogue echoed within the confines of the tiny space.

Thomas closed his eyes and placed his hands to his temples as his head reverberated. It felt as if a jackhammer pounded between his ears.

Joe flung a towel in his direction. "Get cleaned up! You smell like a stinkin' brewery, lad. Come out to the kitchen when you're done. I'm off to find you a new shirt to wear. And put some pants on!"

Joe turned away in disgust, but not before cranking the knob of the shower to the "on" position.

Thomas dropped his briefs on the bathroom floor, flinging

aside the shower curtain. He stepped into the coldest shower he'd ever taken.

"Judas Priest!" he cried out.

But to his credit, he didn't budge or change the water setting. Reaching for the soap, he let the cold water pelt his torso. It was the only way to lift the booze fog from his brain. He braved the icy water as his penance for the night before, then turned the knob to a warmer setting for the last few minutes. Stepping out of the shower to dry off, he found his suit pants hanging on a hook on the back of the bathroom door. They'd been slightly pressed and looked better than they had on the chaise in the bedroom. He slid his legs into the dark trousers, zipped up his pants and scanned the bathroom for his belt, but didn't find it.

Wiping the steamy mirror with his towel, Thomas took a good look at himself. Joe was right. He was a sorry mess. Dropping the wet towel onto the tile floor, he opened the door and walked down the hallway that led to the open living area.

As he slowly made his way down the corridor, he tried to recall the details of the embezzlement scheme. However, the woman who'd stood before him with her hands on her hips, her eyes locked on his as if to say, "What do you think of me now?" kept creeping into his thoughts, undoing his focus. He was flabbergasted at the change in her. She was captivatingly tall, lean, and if he didn't miss his guess, under those clothes, had one hell of a toned body. One that was ripe for making love…again. Thomas stopped briefly, stunned by the fact that even with everything going on, in the middle of this crisis, his primary focus was her. Squirt. Courtney. She'd returned!

Moving down the hall, he thought of how badly he'd bungled things. Thomas regretted what he'd said every day since. And if he could have found her, he would have begged, pleaded and, yes, groveled for her to forgive him. But Courtney bolted from Hampton Beach like a horse out of the starting gate. He had tried everything, including enlisting the farm's security detail to track her down. Rick had been no help. He'd been dealing with a family in crisis that had lost a loving sister and nurturer.

When he approached his Aunt Elizabeth, she shut him out cold. "Your love life is not an international incident, Thomas. Hire a private investigator."

But last night, as if in a dream, Courtney had surfaced from wherever she'd hidden herself and stood right in front of him! Hot, sexy, her black eyes flashing fire. Recalling her jet black hair and its silky texture, he longed to thrust his fingers through her tresses and pull her hard against him.

Unfortunately, from the expression on her face and her body language, he was the last person she wanted to see.

Arriving in the doorway to the kitchen, Thomas expected to find Joe waiting with the promised remainder of clothes to wear and a strong cup of black coffee. But the man was nowhere to be found. The open concept living area housed a stellar, modern kitchen, which was empty. A clean, crisply ironed shirt on a hanger dangled from one of the pulls to a kitchen drawer.

A note, written in Joe's shaky penmanship, was taped to the cabinet above:

There's coffee in the Keurig. Get yourself together. Rick and Courtney's ETA is thirty minutes. I'll be up with your breakfast soon. J.

Looking around the kitchen, Thomas spied what appeared to be an odd kind of appliance on the counter. He walked over to the strange contraption. *So this is a Keurig. Great. Another techno-gismo. I just want a damn cup of black coffee with a dram of Baileys to chase away the hair of the dog that bit me.*

But then he saw a Post-it note attached to one of the three

buttons and smiled. A large mug was strategically placed underneath the drip spout. God bless Joe for setting things up. Thomas read the note. *"Push here, idiot. Court."*

The woman had drawn a cute smiley face under her signature. So that was the way things were going to be, he thought to himself. The note made things perfectly clear. Courtney was definitely *not* happy to be here.

Well, he hadn't been born a Hallock for nothing. Come hell or high water, once he figured out how Courtney figured into Rick's plan, Thomas was dead set on winning her back.

CHAPTER ELEVEN

Courtney made her way down the side alley of the pub. She was about to swing the door open in order to make for the back staircase, but her brother managed to grab hold of her shoulder.

"Stop!" The man had trailed at her back as she half-walked, half-jogged back to the safe house from the coffee shop.

Courtney halted, turning to look Rick in the eye. He was bent over at the waist, hands on his knees, glancing up at her. His eyes seemed to be pleading with her to let him catch his breath, but she had no intention of doing so. "No. We're not having a private conversation out here. Besides, Joe, you and I have a lot of explaining to do to that man waiting upstairs."

She knew where the direction of her brother's conversation was headed. To talk her out of her, how had he called it — "half-brained idea." After much soul searching, her gut reinforced her plan as the perfect cover. She'd have access to everywhere she'd need to go: Tom's office, the Hallock estate and his private home. As his fiancée, no one would question her appearance. Courtney promptly shut down any opportunity Rick had to rebut her by opening the outer door. Once inside, she made for the stairs and started to climb them, taking the steps two at a time.

"You're nuts, you know." Rick obviously had caught his second wind and was right on her heels again. "The Director is *never* going to agree with the idea of you becoming his fiancée. Neither will Tom."

As her foot hit the final step on the fourth floor, she stopped and turned to glance at the man behind her. Rick practically ran into her. She poked a finger into his chest. "You leave the Director to me. Have you forgotten how she loves to play matchmaker? Remember Kate and John? Matt and Megan?" Her brother hesitantly nodded. "She'll say 'yes' in a heartbeat. Mark my words."

Now, maybe he'll quit hounding me, and we can move on!

Courtney continued, "I've no intention of sharing what I have planned for him until we're out in Southampton. He'll see reason when he's been given a rational explanation. Correct me if I'm wrong, but did you not tell me last night Tom hired you to solve this case? He has to let you do what's best. Will he *ever* know I work for the Agency? I hope not. But Tom's not stupid. Last night he found out I'm a cop. We have to insist he sees how imperative it is that everyone be told I left my job at my firm's London office, and at some point it rolled into a job with the FBI. Period."

Courtney turned and made her way down the hall to her apartment door. *What was Rick's problem? The plan made perfect sense. Or had she crossed the line with her idea? No, it was the only plausible way to insert herself back into the Hamptons undetected from the life she'd been living.*

Reaching the door, she pulled a lanyard out from under her tee shirt and drew it over her head.

As she was about to place the key in the lock, Rick laid his hand on top of hers. "Before you open that door, you clearly better understand one thing."

She looked up to see a serious look that matched the tone in his voice. "What?"

"This operation was set up with *me* running point. *You* work for *me*. And as much as I think your idea is absurd, I have to admit you're on to something that actually might work to our advantage." A small semblance of a smile returned to his face. "Open the damn door. I have a feeling there's going to be a hell of a showdown at the Red Lion Corral."

* * *

Hearing voices at the door, Thomas hastily threw on the shirt Joe left for him and pushed the button on the coffee machine. Rick and Courtney were back. He quickly tried to button up his shirt, but his trembling fingers failed him. He wasn't sure if it was leftover fumbling from the night before or the fact he was going to have to face the love of his life sober. He gave up, leaving his shirt wide open. Reaching for the mug, he thought he could put on a good front even though he felt like crap.

"Rick, look what the cat dragged in." Courtney's eyes pierced his own. "Nice of you to take up the *whole* bed *this* time."

Over Courtney's shoulder, Thomas caught Rick's eyebrows arch, shocked at the sexual inference. If he had to explain to his best friend what went down eleven years ago, he'd rather the farm went under.

Thomas managed to mumble, "Morning." He pointed to the Keurig. "Finally figured out how that contraption worked. I don't have one at the office. Quite an invention." He saw Courtney's mouth turn up at its corners.

Deciding it was better to look like he was getting ready, he busied himself by wrapping his hands around the wider than normal coffee cup. Raising it to his lips, he took a liberal swallow of the hot, black liquid. Still somewhat in a fog, he let his senses take over. Damn! Not only had the coffee burned his tongue, but it scalded his throat on the way to his stomach. The cup felt as if it was melting a hole in the palm of his hand. In an act of self-preservation, Thomas released the cup. It hit the hard floor, shattering into tiny pieces.

"Oh, for the love of...." Courtney rushed to where he stood. "Don't move an inch!" He watched as her eyes searched the floor. She glared up at him. "You don't have any shoes on. Stay still! I'll clean this up. Rick, get the broom in that closet." She pointed to a corner cupboard.

Trying to be of help, Thomas bent to retrieve the larger pieces of china around him. But a firm hand pushed him back against the kitchen counter.

"Didn't I just tell you not to touch anything?" Courtney's tone was harsh.

Rick came back with the requested broom, along with a dustpan and handed them to his sister. A sheaf of paper towels in hand, Courtney squatted to mop up the hot liquid before sweeping up the remnants of the broken cup. As she pushed the pieces of white ceramic into a pile, she sighed with what seemed like a tinge of regret. "Oh, no! Not this one!"

Whatever he'd broken meant a great deal to her. Perhaps, a gift from a former lover? But, why would she keep a precious token here?

"Courtney, I'm really sorry." No response. The woman kept blotting spilled coffee and gathering up the shards. "I seem to have made a mess of everything. Look, it's just a mug. I'll buy you another. Okay?"

Courtney stopped what she was doing. "It can't be replaced. It was given to me by - "

She was stopped from completing her thought when Rick's phone rang. Tom watched him glance at the screen. Rick's brow furrowed, and his mouth turned into a frown. Waving the phone in the air, he announced, "I've got to take this. Back in a sec."

With Rick gone, Tom tried to restart their conversation. "Well, the cup is certainly different than any I've seen. Where did you get it?" Thomas was definitely intrigued to see why that particular treasure seemed to arouse a sentimental reaction.

After dumping the last pieces of ceramic and soggy paper towels into a garbage can, she turned and leaned against the counter opposite him. "Forget it. I…ah…I picked it up one day when I went into a shop in London for high tea. The rarity of the size and shape caught my eye. I knew it would keep me on task at my desk at the office. Luckily, the owner had a small gift shop as well, so I purchased a set. End of story."

London, was it? Tea coupled with a blue suit? I'd stake my next dividend check she's acquired my aunt's taste for Earl Grey.

"So you've left your globe-hopping job and become a cop? I see where your background in forensics sort of goes with the sleuthing skills needed by a police department, but - "

Thomas stopped, hearing running footsteps in the hallway. Both he and Courtney turned to see Rick standing at the doorway.

"Courtney, pack your bag ASAP. Thomas, we need to get you dressed. We don't have much time. Joe will be up to give us a quick briefing before we leave."

"Leave for where?" Both Thomas and Courtney chimed in unison.

"For home. We're not going to have time to stay and plan here. My team already has their marching orders from Joe and the Director."

"I'm still not following. What the hell has happened?" Thomas asked. As he did so, a serious look of concern crossed Courtney's face. *She knows something.*

Rick delivered the bad news. "There's been a major break-in at your office. We need to get on your plane once we're done with Joe and fly back to Gabreski. The Chief of STPD will meet us there, along with Geoff Daniels from the farm. We'll head directly to the office. You'll be able to take a look and determine if anything's missing."

Shocked, Thomas spit out, "Where the hell was my staff?"

Rick shrugged his shoulders. "Jim says the computer system crashed. Since it would take time to get rebooted, Hailey told her crew to take an extended lunch break. They're being questioned."

Thomas felt his blood pressure rising. "What does Hailey have to say?"

Rick looked him directly in the eye. "That's where there's a tiny bit of problem. Apparently, Hailey hasn't come back from lunch. Jim thinks she might be AWOL."

CHAPTER TWELVE

Hallock Farm Office
Southampton, New York
Three p.m.

W hen the Hallock's company jet landed at Gabreski Airport in Hampton Beach, Rick hopped into a police car driven by Jim Benjamin and sped off toward Sunrise Highway, leaving Courtney standing alone on the tarmac with Thomas. A black Town Car immediately pulled up, and the two piled into its backseat for the thirty-minute ride.

The distraught look on his face was her undoing. But, she had remained silent during the ride in the jet to the Hampton Beach airport. She'd been surprised he had not a bombarded her with myriad of questions about her present or past doings.

As the Town Car took off, the man sitting on her right leaned back in the comfortable black leather seat and stared out the window, deep in thought. Perhaps his silence would give her the time she desperately needed to collect her thoughts. Personally, Courtney's take was Thomas was in a state of shock and denial due given the short timeframe he'd had to digest the known information regarding the embezzlement scam. She couldn't imagine his reaction when the time came to inform him of their overall plan.

Now, standing in the middle of Hailey Rockwell's office, her eyes scanned every nook and cranny, looking for clues. Hailey was still missing and considering what happened to Janie, both she and Rick were concerned. The less Thomas knew about that, though, the better. He was far more rational and easier to deal with when given specifics facts. And far less likely to question or interfere in the ongoing investigation.

Walking out of the office, she spied Rick, Thomas, Jim and Jack Jessop, the new CEO, gathered near the door that led to the large room where Hailey's assistants worked in small cubicles. That area had been trashed. The CSU, according to Jim Benjamin, had been over every inch of the offices.

"Anything catch your eye?" Rick stepped slightly away from the group, his voice a hushed whisper.

She looked around at the chaos. With gloves on her hands, she reached for several pieces of paper stuck in a printer. More invoices. Were they real or fabricated? "I can't comprehend, if the staff was gone for ninety minutes, why the laptops and computers weren't taken in the B&E. In her book, it points to somebody looking for something specific." She turned and addressed the CEO, who stood talking to Thomas. "Jack, what about your office?"

"It looks as if whoever did this just decided to turn my desk upside-down for show. My laptop's trashed. I don't get it. Maybe you guys can piece together what went on. I'm not a cop, but I will say, my gut says things don't add up."

It had been a long time since Courtney had seen Jack Jessop. He'd been friends with her brother and Tom since the three played on the golf team in high school. Surprise had registered on his face when she'd appeared at the scene. The Director had given Rick the go-ahead to allow Jack into their inner circle, but only divulge she was employed currently with the FBI's bureau office in New York City.

"I agree. Someone was looking for something." Rick walked to Jack's doorway where Courtney had already studied the damage. "Your filing cabinets were rifled or made to look that way. What did you store in them?"

"Nothing but paper files on clients. Kate had a system she liked to use. Hailey was training the staff to put all those files into the new computer system so we'd have backup to the Cloud. Then, we'd use Dropbox to obtain the files when needed for updating. Tom and I didn't have a problem with her going ahead with the idea, as long as she guaranteed we have a high level of security. In order to be efficient, we had to modernize the office to keep up with the demands of the training facility and the rehab center. Hallock Farm has and is growing, especially since Kate introduced all those new veterinary methods. Tom and I thought it a must. The Board concurred."

Thomas broke in. "Well, what's next? Did anything happen to my apartment upstairs or my home?"

Jim answered, "No. My officers checked. Nothing's disturbed. I'm a little surprised that there wasn't any attempt to break in upstairs. I think the perps ran out of time, or someone scared them off."

Courtney had had an in-depth discussion with the Chief of STPD and her brother. She wasn't convinced this was a legitimate B&E. It didn't seem to have the right feel. It felt staged. "Has anyone checked the information on the server?"

"Andrew and Troy are doing that right now." Courtney noted Rick didn't inform anyone his IT people were already in place at her family's home. Her brother turned to Jim. "When will you be finished taking statements? We need to concentrate on finding Hailey."

"Shouldn't be much longer. What do you want me to tell your staff when my men are done?"

Courtney saw the frustration cross Thomas's face as he paced the carpet. "You really shouldn't be in here, Tom. We need to get you home and into some clean clothes. You need to assure your parents everything is under control. Word will have reached the estate. Knowing Robert and Helen, they'll be concerned for you and the business. Your mother will be frantic."

Thomas acknowledged her remarks with a nod, but addressed his question to the Chief of Police. "Jim, you mentioned the CSU was finished? I have a few things I want to look for. I planted a few false items in my office before I left yesterday."

"Come again?" Jim seemed to be caught off-guard.

He folded his arms over his puffed-up chest. "I inputted a few fake files and attached invoices." Thomas looked as if he was going to take on the Chief of Police in the middle of the hallway.

Courtney eyed the police chief carefully, looking for micro-expressions. A small tic occurred in the corner of his eye at Thomas's revelation. Interesting, Courtney thought to herself. The man knows something we don't.

Jim cleared his throat as if to regroup. "Yeah, Tom, they're done. Go ahead and look. I've got to go see how my men made out."

Rick and Jim had commandeered the café across the street for questioning the employees. Since the establishment wasn't heavily used at this time of the year, Rick had paid the owner a handsome fee to shut down for the day.

As Jim walked out the door, Thomas turned back to face Jack, Courtney and Rick. "My sixth sense tells me there's more to this break-in than what it appears to look like. This was a set-up to get my staff out of here. Any of you agree?"

Courtney had similar thoughts, but kept them to herself. "Maybe. Rick, shouldn't we put out an APB for Hailey? Jim didn't say one word about searching for her. Don't you think that's odd? Someone had to see her leave for lunch. Do you think there's a possibility she's been kidnapped?"

Rick frowned. "Excuse us." Rick pulled on her arm to take her out of earshot of Thomas and Jack. "Okay, I agree. But Jim said no APB. Tell you what. Call Sarah Adams. Do you think Matt will have a problem with her taking some time, since it's not officially beach season?"

Sarah Adams, the manager of the Sunfish Beach Club, was also a CIA operative. Unknown to Thomas's brother, Matt, the owner, but not to his wife, Megan, herself an operative, Sarah had proved herself to the Director during Operation Hurricane. She'd be perfect to infiltrate throughout the villages and seek out the information needed.

"I'll make contact. She's got great cover connections. Joe knows her well. We'd be wise to use her as a conduit."

Hearing the front door open, all heads turned to see who'd entered the cordoned-off area marked with police tape.

"What the hell happened to my office?" The feminine voice shrieked, distress showing on the new arrival's face.

Hailey Rockwell had returned from lunch—very, very, late.

* * *

Courtney stood looking through the glass of the interrogation room at Hailey Rockwell. The little the woman saw of her, the better. Hailey returned from her lunch break to find Rick, Thomas and Jim debating the crime scene, with Courtney added to the mix. Rick had the forethought to immediately step in, seeing the woman's questioning stare, introducing her as his sister. At that point, both Rick and Jim decided to head to the police station on the off-chance the office was bugged.

In Courtney's opinion, Hailey had reached her breaking point. In the short time since her return, Jim had grilled Hailey with a vengeance. It had to be done, but there were better ways to interrogate his witness, Courtney thought. Hailey dabbed at her eyes when given tissues only to sob uncontrollably again.

"Once more, Miss Rockwell." Jim didn't let up. "The timing of the break-in is just too perfect. You have a set routine I'm told. You go to lunch practically the same time every day. True?"

"Well, yes. We all take our lunch breaks around noon. Look. I don't know how much more I can tell you. We started the training session around ten. I gave my staff files that contained information on horses run at Belmont, which were now out for stud. I was showing them how to use the new system to input each horse's statistics into the database, how to save it and... poof! I shouted to try to back up the files when the computer screens began to flash, but it was too late. The laptops went dark."

"Everyone's? Yours, as well?" Rick's tone had more settling and soothing tone in his voice.

"Of course, mine!" she countered. "Are you accusing me of something?"

Courtney was perturbed neither man followed the questions from her "playbook." Hailey had been more than cooperative. If the two pressed her much longer, the woman would be demanding an attorney.

Rick lay his pen down on the legal pad on the table. "Understand we're trying to line up the facts. Did anything seem out of the ordinary this morning?"

The woman looked up, glancing toward the plate glass window, as if she could see Courtney. "No. It's like I've said. My answers aren't going to change, gentlemen." Suddenly, she sat up straight. "Are you hounding me because of who my brother is?"

Courtney eyes darted in her brother's direction and then subtly glanced at Jim. The Chief slid out of the metal chair on which he'd been sitting the last half hour and stood. He paced around the table, circling Hailey as if to taunt her, intimidate her. *Interesting. Where was the man going with his tactic? Whatever he was planning sure as hell wasn't working.*

As far as Courtney was concerned, they'd all be better to reschedule for tomorrow. Let Hailey regroup. She could slip up. Change her story. Or forget something.

She exited the viewing room into the hallway. Everyone was on edge and had to remain calm. Against her better judgment, Courtney entered the interrogation room. Heads turned. The glare Jim shot her way told her he was none too pleased to see her.

Courtney walked toward Hailey and rested her hip on the corner of the table. She said reassuringly, "Hailey, you got this job on your own merits. You were thoroughly vetted or you wouldn't be head CPA. Relax a bit. This interrogation is strictly protocol. Rick and Jim do it with every case. Your brother and his..." She grasped for the proper words. "...*activities* have nothing to do with you." She glanced down and leveled a look at the obviously nervous woman. "You've told us everything you can think of for now?"

Hailey nodded her head. Meekly, twisting a tissue in her hand, she said, "Yes."

"Jim? Rick? Have you got what you need for now?" Courtney knew the time had come to let the woman go. "Rick, how 'bout a bodyguard?" Hailey had started to rise from the metal chair, but Courtney placed a hand on the woman's shoulder to stop her from getting up and leaving.

"No!" Jim's snapping tone took Courtney by surprise,

considering the Director was springing for extra security. The large burly man leaned over the table and pointed his finger at the woman who sat there. "Text your staff. Tell them not to return to the office today. It's still a working crime scene. Tomorrow, you can speak to Mr. Hallock."

"I can do that." The woman nodded, her voice shaking in compliance. She took one look at Courtney and rose slowly from her chair. Once at the door, she quickly fled the room.

"What the hell do you think you're doing waltzing in here like that?" Rick sounded as pissed as Jim. "You could compromise everything. I don't need her thinking you're a cop."

Courtney looked at Jim before she countered her brother's accusation. "Let me refresh your memory. That woman saw me inside Tom's office. You introduced me as your sister. She has no idea where I was before I walked into the room."

Jim placed his hands on the table and eyed her suspiciously. "So you *really* are a cop? I thought you were coming back to Hampton Beach because you'd given up your cushy, international CPA job from too much stress."

Play it carefully. "I told Rick I didn't want to publicize why I came back. I've been in New York for a few months. I picked up a side job working as a forensics accountant for the FBI. The temp job turned into full-time. I like it. Rick borrowed me three days ago from the Bureau when things started imploding regarding Tom's situation. I had three weeks of vacation coming to me, so here I am."

Jim, arms crossed, eyed her warily.

"What's wrong?" Courtney asked, seeing the flashes of doubt cross his face.

Jim snorted, "Just what I need. More cops to get in the way of the job I have to do. Your brother and I have things under control."

Rick interjected, "Another pair of eyes never hurt, Jim. You know that. My sister may be an asset when it comes to Hailey. She's going to work on the case, whether you like it or not." From the glare in Jim's eyes, her brother had rubbed the chief the wrong way.

In order to ease the tension, Courtney yawned and rubbed her neck. "I say we get out of here. We need to get Tom home. The man's dead on his feet."

The two men nodded at each other, finally in agreement. Rick opened the door and motioned for Courtney to go ahead of him down the hallway.

Nearing the Chief's office she saw Thomas sitting in the overstuffed, leather chair behind the desk. Knocking softly, he opened one eye as she entered.

In a hushed whisper, she said, "Sorry to wake you. It's time to get you home."

"Finally! I packed up a few bags to take to my house."

"You mean your parents'," Courtney countered.

"No." Thomas's voice grew defiant as he rose out from the chair. "I'm going *home*. To *my* house on the ocean. I want to sleep in my own bed, hear the waves crashing on the beach as I go to sleep. It'll bring me some peace from what I've been through the last couple of days."

"Hmnn… I think that will be okay with my brother. Let's get your bags into the Town Car. Rick is right behind us. I'll text him the change in plans."

She shot off a message to Rick as Thomas picked up two suitcases and made for the front door of the police station. His chauffeur was waiting outside with the trunk open. Courtney practically ran into him when he came up short.

"Whose bags are those?" Thomas spun around, pointing to three Louis Vuitton pieces of luggage parked on the steps.

Courtney smiled, a wide grin on her face. She couldn't help it. She'd bested the man at his own game.

"No! Absolutely not! I forbid it!"

"Hush up!" She smacked him on the shoulder. "Do you want everyone in town knowing your business? Whether you like it or not, Thomas, you need someone to guard you inside the house. The perimeter's covered, but Jim's officers are stretched thin around town. Your aunt and Geoff Daniels hired coverage for the entire farm area and outside your house. But…"

"No, Squirt. I want to be alone. Besides, I've got a gun. I can use it if I have to."

Courtney wasn't going to be deterred. *Was the man in for the surprise of a lifetime.* "The size of your estate poses a big problem. Have you given any thought that someone can get at you from the beach?"

Thomas blanched and slowly his hands shot up above his head. "Okay. Okay. I'm too tired to fight anymore. I give up. But, you, lady, will take one wing, and I'll take the other. Got it?"

Crossing her fingers behind her back, Courtney replied, "Works for me."

With the bags stowed in the trunk of the car, the two hopped in the back and headed out of town to Tom's mansion on the beach.

* * *

The silence inside the car made Courtney acutely aware of the buzz of leaf blowers and the drone of lawn mowers as they drove past the magnificent properties where groundskeepers prepared the residences for the summer season. The older Hampton estates were surrounded by privet hedges at least six to eight feet high. She could tell as the car passed by the multitude of houses, the number of landscapers required to do one estate reached crowd-level. It was a booming business.

Courtney had no idea where Thomas's home was situated. Trying to seem as if she were making casual conversation, she asked, "So where is this mansion?"

"Just up ahead."

The driver slowed, turning the Town Car onto a massive brick driveway. After pressing in a pass code that opened an eight foot tall rustic wooden gate, the car began its journey, passing a large amount of flowerbeds packed with hydrangeas and lilies. At the end of the long brick drive stood a large white mansion. Its columns supported both the upper and lower floors at the entryway. An enormous wraparound deck on both tiers was perfect for taking in the ocean views at any time of day.

Courtney gasped. Her left hand rested on her heart as her right held onto the seat. She leaned toward Thomas for a closer view out his window. *No! It wasn't possible! This was the house! The house she'd told him she'd love to raise a family in on that night so very long ago. The Gin Lane House!*

All of a sudden she felt the warmth of his hand covered hers.

"Like it, Court? I've had some work done to it."

Like it? What an understatement! She couldn't wait to see inside. What did this mean? Girl, you got to keep your focus.

Courtney's primary purpose for being in Southampton was to do the job she'd been assigned to do. The last thing she wanted was to answer to an angry Director. *Oh, Thomas! What have you done to me again?*

CHAPTER THIRTEEN

Eckart's Luncheonette
Hampton Beach

"What the hell are we doing meeting here, of all places? It's way too public." Jim Benjamin sounded as if he'd gotten out of the wrong side of the bed that morning. Hell, since they'd all returned to Hampton Beach and met back up with Jim, the man had sounded "off". By the looks of the man sitting opposite him, Rick would gamble the cop hadn't been to bed yet either. He hadn't shaved, and his shirt and pants were wrinkled. Not the Jim Benjamin he knew. No wonder he wanted a place more private.

The Chief of the STPD yanked out the wooden chair of the small round table and sat. Rick had picked the far back corner of the popular breakfast joint on purpose. Jim rattled on, pointing to the counter where the locals gathered for their morning coffee. "I don't want to be the talk of the town in case they overhear what we uncovered."

When Rick called Jim the night before to inform him where to meet, the man pitched a fit. Rick explained everyone would have, by that hour of the morning, read the *Hampton Times*.

Knowledge of the break-in at Tom's office would be making the rounds. But the specifics wouldn't. The paper, based in Southampton, would have a reporter with exclusive access to any of the officers who just might be a "reliable source within the STPD" adding details.

Rick raised his finger to his lips, as if that was going to really help quiet Jim. "You're making way too much out of meeting here. If we start holing up in out-of-the-way places, people are going to read more into what's happened. Everybody knows your face. Remember? Your campaign manager plastered it all over the town's billboards before the November election."

Jim's eyes met his with a dagger-like glare. His badge and ego often got the better of him.

Shirley Eckart, the proprietor, came up to their table just in time. Jim squirmed in his seat. A white apron wrapped around her waist, a pad of paper stuffed in its pocket, she gave Rick a wide smile. She held up the pot of coffee. "Rick, you need a refill?"

"Absolutely." He returned her grin with one of his own. "I'll have an order of chocolate chip pancakes with a side of breakfast sausage."

The woman took a pencil out of the bun on the back of her head and wrote his order down on the pad. She warily eyed his companion. "What about you, Mr. Chief of Police? Going to be cheap and just go for coffee?"

Rick snickered silently. The elderly woman had never forgiven Jim for stealing candy from the counter when they'd been kids. Everyone else had owned up to what they had done. His parents had made him return to the store, pay the money back *and* put him to work his penance off in the store after school. Jim had refused to do the right thing by her and her husband, Red. In the years that passed, Shirley'd never let Jim forget. "I'll go all in today. Apparently, Rick's got a bigger expense account, Shirl."

"That's Mrs. Eckart to you, *Chief*." She turned and quickly walked away from their table, muttering under her breath.

Jim jerked his finger in her direction. "That woman has hated me my entire life. See why I didn't want to come here?"

Jim's attitude had worn thin. "Get off your high horse and leave the past to rest. Look, I don't have much time. Tell me what your CSU team uncovered." Rick put two scoops of sugar in his black coffee and raised the cup to his lips.

Jim picked up the knife from the place setting and twirled it in his hand. "Zip. Nada. Not one fingerprint in the place. Hailey is spending this morning with her staff going through the paper files. Tom's office has to shut down for a few days."

From his perspective, Rick believed yesterday's job hadn't been carried out by a pro. The total lack of fingerprints didn't point in that direction. The two pieces of information didn't jive.

In addition, he'd been to the Stockton house to check in on Troy and Andrew. The two were knee-deep into writing code that apparently, since the security had been breached at the farm's office, allowed them to hack in and retrieve the passwords of the accounts that had been previously changed. Troy, as usual had very little to say, just nodding when asked a question. Andrew, on the other hand, interpreted what they'd accomplished in layman's terms so Rick would understand. Andrew felt that small glitch of time was a major break in following the cyber trail to where the money was diverted. But as he pointed out, the minute the computers began working again, firewalls flew up, stopping the progress made.

"Where's Tom in all of this?" Rick asked, knowing there was no way he was going to impart the inner network of the team he'd established with Jim. Sixth sense, told him not to and after texting Court, she agreed.

Jim sipped his coffee and placed his cup on the table. "I spoke with Tom this morning. Obviously, he wants to return to the office. I told him to let Hailey and her team get their bearings. I'd be sure there was security round the clock. He's going to check in around mid-afternoon."

"He was okay with that?" Rick couldn't believe Tom caved so easily, given the fact he was so hyped up over the case two days before. Maybe Courtney was having the desired calming effect they'd hoped for. He sure would have loved to have seen the look on his best friend's face when she announced she was accompanying him *to his house* and acting as his bodyguard.

"Seems to be. There is one problem, though."

The teenage waitress showed up at their table, cutting off Rick's reply. She served them their breakfasts. He smiled up at the teenager.

"That's all," Jim stated gruffly, waving her off. The girl walked away.

What an ass Jim could be, Rick thought. "A problem? Exactly what would that be?"

"Sammy. Rick, I tried pulling him in off the street. Geoff tried talking to him. Said we could hide him. The kid wouldn't have anything to do with being in a safe house. Said he was better out on the streets, trying to find the nut who'd killed Janie."

Rick stopped chewing his food and laid his fork on his plate. "He said *what?*"

"You heard me."

"What did you do? I hope you didn't let him out of your sight."

Jim stuffed the pancakes into his mouth and struggled to talk with his mouth full. "Got it under control."

Rick hesitated, but had to find out. "What did you do, Jim?"

"We cuffed him and brought him into the station. Told him

he's safer in a cold jail than he is on the street right now. Some tough guy. From the look in his eyes, the kid's scared shit-less since Janie was sliced and diced." Jim leaned over the table and said in a hushed voice, his fork pointing at Rick. "That kid knows something."

On that note, Rick lost his appetite. "I have to talk to him."

"Maybe *you* can reason with him. I sure as hell can't. The minute I walk in the room, he clams up."

"I'll get over to your office sometime this afternoon. I'll text you a time." Rick emptied the last of his coffee, disgusted that he'd learned nothing from Jim. "Anything else you want to share? You're the one who wanted the meeting."

"That sister of yours. Sure surprised the hell out of me coming back to town. First, we hear she washed up and stressed out and bolted from her high-pressure international job. I bet she's seen the world, huh?"

He's fishing for information. Why? Rick merely nodded his head, trying his best to keep a stoic look on his face. It was that damn text from Janie that stopped him from trusting anyone but his sister and his crew and the man he was heading out to meet.

Rick had to keep Courtney's cover hidden and stop Jim's curiosity cold turkey. "You should have seen her when she arrived back in New York. She was a mess - zoned out from the pressure. But, Court's like me. Can't sit still. Had to have something to occupy her time. You know the rest."

Jim leaned back in his chair. "She sure turned into a stunner...not that she wasn't a beauty in high school."

Rick grew tired with Jim's idle chit-chat. He looked at his watch. Their meeting had been a total waste of time. Jim had given him nothing new, other than the fact Sammy was sitting in the Southampton jail. He had to talk to the kid. Try to make him see reason. What was Sammy thinking? Now, he really needed to contact his sister. She'd have a spin on Sammy's situation and what to do about it.

As he was searching for a plausible excuse to bring this sorry meeting to an end, the waitress showed up with the bill for breakfast. Perfect timing.

Jim stood, putting on his coat and placing his hat on his head. "Give the check to him. He's paying." He shot the teenager a grin, which wasn't returned. She slapped a piece of paper into the palm of his hand. Perplexed, he asked, "What's this?"

As the girl picked up their plates and cups and placed them on a tray, she said saucily, "That's for you from Mrs. Eckart. It's the money you owe her for the candy...plus interest. She said to tell you you're lucky the rates are at an all-time low." She hefted the tray of dirty dishes onto her shoulders and walked away.

Rick couldn't help but laugh out loud. "You had it coming. Admit it."

Jim's face grew as red as a beet. "Text me," he growled. He stormed off past the locals sitting at the counter. Rick watched them wave good-bye behind Jim's back as the door slammed shut behind him.

* * *

Jetty 4 Beach
Dune Road
Hampton Beach

Standing on the boardwalk after climbing a flight of stairs, Rick breathed in the harsh, but refreshing smell of the salt sea air. On a normal beach day, sunbathers would flock over the dunes to the ocean on the other side. He realized how much he missed those days of long walks and runs he'd taken with his sister when they were younger. As the eldest boy and girl in the family, they'd meet up here to plan and strategize what they'd do to save the family from financial ruin. It had been a week-to-week challenge.

One day, knowing full well they reached the point of no return, Robert Hallock, Thomas's father, stepped in to help. How the man had come to know of their private family crisis Rick never knew to this day. Rick never shared with Tom how truly bad things had become in the Stockton home. Everyone in town knew their mother was dying of cancer and there was no health insurance for treatments. But the fact they lived each day with an abusive, alcoholic father was kept a dark family secret.

The Hallocks, both Robert and Helen, along with Robert's sister, Elizabeth, had generously donated a serious sum of money to a bank account which only he and Courtney could access. It had literally saved him and his siblings. His friendship with Tom and the fact that the Hallocks had done what they did to aid his family were the primary reasons he and Courtney were back to save Hallock Farm.

Hearing the sound of a car's tires travel over broken sea shells on the pavement behind him sent Rick to seek shelter on the other side of the dunes among the grasses. The man was punctual.

Footsteps pounded on the staircase. Before long, a surfer in a black wet suit appeared with his board chained to his wrist. He looked up and down the beach.

Seeing no one in sight, the man called out, "Rick, you here?"

Rick stood up in the tall grasses. "Dan. Thanks for coming. I like your disguise. Going in?"

Dan McVey stared back at Rick. "You nuts? One, it's too freaking cold. And two, you know very well I don't swim."

Rick chuckled, moving closer. "Come on. Leave your board. We'll walk a ways down the beach. I cased the area. I didn't see anyone." He shivered and pulled the lapel of his peacoat up around his neck to ward off the brisk wind.

"I don't have as much time as I thought. The roster changed. I only have an hour to get back to my house and head to a briefing at HBPD. There's a big bust going down, and the chief moved up my time to report."

"I only need a few minutes. Were you able to get a read on the photos of those two men from the bar at the St. Regis?"

Dan unzipped the top of his wet suit and pulled out two grainy photos. "I hope you're not planning on side-lining as a photographer." The young man laughed. "But you were in luck. I was able to make IDs. The big guy on the left is Harry Thorton. He's got a sheet a mile long but nothing big. Larceny, B&E. No weapons charges. The other geeky guy took awhile. It was the glasses that kept throwing the facial recognition software off. When I deleted the frames using Photoshop, bingo! A nine-point match. Carl Jackson. For a geek, he's got a pretty impressive criminal resume. He's done some time for assault and B&E. He's been on Interpol's and the FBI's watch list for over a year."

"I don't get how the two are connected."

"Neither did I until I remembered a case back in the Bronx last year. I got sent to find a suspect we'd been searching for after a series of robberies - stolen jewelry and, more important, webcams and laptops. The officers who had jurisdiction on the case told me they had Jason Rockwell and two of his companies under surveillance for four months. The department was about to place four officers undercover within his organization. This geek works for Rockwell. Get this. He's got a degree from MIT with a major in computer programming and a minor in art. Convenient, no? Interpol's tracking him for hacking into bank accounts, but also looking at him for stealing several well-known pieces of artwork in Europe. My contact says he'd left a trail and he's selling on the black market. Wouldn't have thought it by the looks of him."

Jason Rockwell? How could it be possible? Tom's aunt had assured us Hailey was clean.

Rick's mind began to whirl with the information he'd just been given, coupling it with what he already knew. Courtney had even reiterated from her briefings with Sam Tanner that she'd been told Hailey separated from her brother and set out to make a legit life for herself.

Rick felt a slap on the back.

Danny McVey looked concerned. "You okay? You look as if you've just been plowed over by a steamroller."

"Ah, yeah. This puts a different spin on things related to the case, considering his sister's working in Tom's office." Rick replied. "I owe you."

"If I find out anything else, I'll let you know. With this new case, you might not be able to reach me, but in an emergency you know who to contact."

"I do. I can take it from here. Appreciate the help, though. I don't have to warn you to keep the info close to the vest."

"You know I will."

The two men shook hands, and Rick watched the man trek up the beach and pick up his surfboard. When the man's head disappeared over the dunes, Rick turned and faced the ocean. High tide was rolling in. The waves had increased in intensity. He was in desperate need of a caffeine jolt. Taking his iPhone out of his pocket, he sent off a coded text. It was imperative the two of them put their heads together to figure out how they were going to deal with the possibility that Jason Rockwell had climbed to the top of his list of suspects. And not just for what was happening with the farm. The man might have had someone off Janie Walker.

As he turned to make his way toward the boardwalk, he

was reminded how the beach had always given him a sense of peace, a tranquil place to contemplate. Today that idea seemed ironic.

Now, as the dark clouds moved in from the south and the waves slammed onto the shore, Rick found himself fearful for the first time in his life. He prayed he'd do the right thing. That he and Courtney would be able to stop the madness before something awful happened to his best friend and his family.

CHAPTER FOURTEEN

Southampton

The brightness that poured into the bedroom from the large windows caused Courtney to squint her eyes as she awoke to face a new day. Easing herself up on her elbows, she surveyed the Nantucket-themed room. The ceiling's clapboard paneling was painted a bright white and the four walls, a robin's egg blue. The interior decorator's fee must have cost a bundle. The mixture of modern and antique furniture, the colors, and the selected mix-and-match pillows, brought the room's beach theme to life.

Swinging her legs over the side of the four-poster, king-sized bed, she took in the ocean view from the second story bedroom. The waves crashed onto the shore, water rushing up the sand, leaving foam and seaweed in its wake. The American flag Thomas erected at the end of the patio that surrounded the outdoor salt-water pool flapped hard from the wind blowing in from the north. No doubt it was cold outside. She'd longed for a morning run when she collapsed, tired and worn, into bed the night before. She'd have to work off her frustrations and get her mind set for the day by using the treadmill in Thomas's fitness room.

A special ringtone blared in the room, and she reached for her encrypted cell, recognizing Rick as the caller. She swiped in her access code and stared at the time on the screen. Eleven a.m! He would have been up for hours and pissed she hadn't been ready to go at the crack of dawn. She couldn't stop yawning, her body still not recovered from days of limited amounts of shuteye.

Putting the phone to her ear, she tried to sound cheerful, not weary. "Good morning. Before you go off half-cocked, I know I should have checked in earlier. I didn't expect to sleep so late. What's up?"

Rick replied, "It's okay. You needed the rest. We didn't really afford you the time to get adjusted to jet lag and get a good night's sleep. Listen, I just met with a reliable source. A few issues surfaced. I need to talk to you in private. It can't be anywhere close to home or in Southampton."

"That bad?" Courtney sat up straight, her curiosity piqued.

"Might be. Did you get a chance to talk to Sarah Adams yesterday?"

"No. I had my hands full with Tom. The man was none too pleased at my taking up residence as his bodyguard at his beach house."

"Did you talk to him about your cover yet?"

"No. I'll do that this morning. He barely spoke to me over dinner. Just kept staring at me. My coming back has definitely caught him off-guard. I don't think he's buying the fact that I work for the FBI."

A small grin formed at the corners of her mouth as she remembered her arrival at Casa de Hallock. When the car stopped, Thomas opened his door and went running up the steps. Left at the curb with the chauffeur, she watched his back as he entered the house without her. As Courtney climbed up the steps to the front door, she heard him yelling for Natasha, the housekeeper. The woman retaliated in Russian. Courtney, who spoke five languages fluently, clearly understood the woman's displeasure. Natasha ranted at him, giving him a piece of her mind.

"Courtney! Court!" The sound of her brother's voice brought her back to the present. "You there? Wake up. Have you had any contact with Sarah?"

"No, sorry, Rick. I crashed. I'll get in touch. I have to go through certain channels. You sound stressed."

"No kidding. Listen, there's a major problem we hadn't planned on. We need to figure out how to solve it. You know where to meet up."

"What time?" Thinking of what she had on her checklist for the day, Courtney prayed Sarah was available to get over to the North Shore and have Rick fill her in.

Her brother sounded frantic. "Around dusk. Six o'clock. Bring her with you. Court, really emphasize how much I'm going to need her. I need an extra set of eyes and ears."

"Rick?"

"Yeah?"

Always the caretaker, she said in a soothing voice, "Take a deep breath. Remember what you told me. It's not an easy case for either one of us. You've brought in your best team. Tom's covered. We'll figure out what's going on tonight and move ahead."

A deep sigh came through the other end of the phone. "Copy that." The phone went dead.

Courtney placed it back on her nightstand, stood up and stretched. There was a knock at the door.

"Yes?" Courtney quickly covered her naked body with a plush bathrobe.

"It's Natasha."

"Come in."

The door opened. An older woman in her forties walked in, bath towels in her hand. She closed the door behind her. Standing approximately five-foot four and possessing a well-toned body, Natasha was dressed in jeans, sturdy sneakers and a white turtleneck top. Her shoulder-length brown hair was pulled back in a ponytail, a hint of gray showed at her ears.

The woman spoke in Russian. "Well, it certainly took you long enough to get here."

Courtney smiled at her former partner. She countered back in Russian, "How long have you been here?"

Switching over to English in case Tom should be passing by outside, Natasha replied, "Eight months." She lowered her voice. "The Director sure has a way about her when handling her nieces and nephews. Thomas was at a family dinner at the estate, and the minute he said he'd bought this house and the construction was nearing completion, the Director was ready with a friend who was letting go a 'housekeeper' and he'd be doing a favor if he hired me."

"Couldn't have planned it better." Courtney took the towels from her friend. "But don't wait on me, Tash. Just do your thing in front of Tom."

"The man's pretty sharp at putting two and two together. The Director heard him at that family dinner say he'd probably been set up. When I had my interview, he was direct. Wanted to know how long I'd known his aunt. His brother, Ethan, was with him. Ethan tried to make a joke about how his aunt always played matchmaker. I began to cuss in Russian, and both their jaws hit the ground. The Director bristled, silencing me with a piercing glare. I'm lucky I'm here because I told him I had no interest in taking the job if he was looking for something more than a housekeeper."

"I can only imagine you were detained and received a severe

dressing down?"

"*Nyet.* The woman knew I'd made my point to clear the air with her nephew. So here I am. Mission semi-accomplished."

Courtney laughed out loud and covered her mouth with her right hand, afraid of being heard. "Agent Tanner gave me an envelope for you on the plane." She walked over to a leather carry-on bag, reached inside and pulled out the gold package. Handing the item over to Natasha, she said, "Everyone's ID is in here. Also, who Raul can let onto the property. Tom doesn't know it yet, but he's not going to have full access to this mansion now that we're all in place. It also has a few assignments for several of the agents on the ground. All the instructions are there."

Suddenly, both women heard heavy footsteps pause in the hallway.

"Mr. Hallock is having breakfast in the nook in the kitchen, Ms. Stockton." Natasha's voice rose in volume, sounding lofty and official.

"Tell him to wait for me, please. I want a shower and then I'll be down. Is there any Earl Grey?"

"All stocked up. Breakfast will be waiting."

The person lurking outside could be heard moving on.

"Tash, did everyone get the supply of ammo for their weapons?"

"Yes. Raul stashed five AK-47's which can be easily accessed. I've got to go. The man's going to wonder why the hell his cook's not in the kitchen making breakfast. It doesn't take this long to deliver towels. We'll figure out how to communicate within the house." She abruptly turned, opened the door and walked out.

Knowing she had little time to spare, Courtney opened the closet, looking for warm clothing to wear. Once in the bathroom, she shed her robe, turned on the shower, tested the temperature of the water and when it turned hot, hopped in. As she lathered up, she wondered what obstacles the day would bring. Turning around and around to get the soap off her body, her mind wandered elsewhere - dreaming of the day Tom would whisk her up in his arms and share an intimate bath with her. With that errant thought playing too vividly in her mind, she reached for the shower knob to set the temperature to cold. The water did its job. Wide awake, but wanting that morning cup of tea and some sustenance, she shut off the faucet and stepped out of the shower, toweling herself dry.

Based on Thomas's demeanor the night before, Courtney had no doubt there would be a showdown at breakfast. She was prepared. But how was he going to take the news that he was about to go from being the Hamptons' most eligible bachelor to a fiancé in the blink of an eye?

* * *

When Courtney walked into the mansion's kitchen, she stopped, stunned. It was the mirror image of the one constructed in Elizabeth Hallock's DC compound. But, she had to be careful. Thomas had no idea she'd been a guest at the woman's home on several occasions in between missions.

A deep voice spoke, startling her. "What are you gaping at? I told you I had the place remodeled."

"It's so, so…." Courtney turned to eye the man sitting in the nook, sipping coffee. The morning edition of the paper lay on the table. She took in his appearance. If she thought he'd exuded sex appeal eleven years ago, he'd aged into one head-turning specimen of a man. His dark hair was still slightly damp from a shower. He wore a pair of khaki pants and a navy blue polo shirt, opened up to the third button. Dark chest hairs were visible. If she didn't stop staring, she'd be a blathering idiot. It was bad enough a warm tingling feeling shot through her body to settle between her legs.

"You going to finish that sentence or just look at me like a dog looks at a bone he can't have?" There was a gleam in Tom's eyes, and the tone in his voice sounded seductive.

Must be the state of my mind…and the naked visual I just had of you in my shower.

"I'm not quite awake yet. Sorry." As she walked over to sit down, she got a better view of the entire kitchen. Elizabeth's kitchen cabinets were cherry. Here, the cabinets looked the same but were painted a glossy white. The beams must have been taken from an old house or barn somewhere nearby. The coffered ceiling added an antique décor to the room. The biggest bay window Courtney ever saw sat over a white soapstone sink and looked out over the backyard, framing the view to the ocean that lay beyond. A large butcher-block island stood in the middle of the room where Natasha was busy preparing their food.

When Courtney sat down, she tried to busy herself by reaching for the paper. Sure enough, the office break-in had made the front page.

Out of the corner of her eye, she caught Thomas staring at her questioningly. "How did you sleep? Any problems?"

"Slept like a baby. Wish I could have had those windows opened though."

"The weather's deceiving. You would have frozen to death. When we leave here, be sure you're dressed warm. Which brings up an issue we have to get out of the way."

Just as she was about to ask what he was referring to, Natasha arrived with their breakfast. Courtney had to hand it to her former partner. The one thing she'd loved about being paired with Tash on an assignment in Russia was the woman could cook - big time. Courtney was lucky she could boil water, but she did operate a microwave dinner pretty damn well. She'd been spoiled in Positano. Salvatore's Italian cook had done everything. She had the extra ten pounds to prove it.

"Thank you. Natasha, is it? May I call you that?" Courtney asked.

"You may." The woman laid on the Russian accent extremely thick. Good.

"Don't get on her bad side or she'll swear at you in Russian." Tom remarked. "Half the time, I don't have any idea what she's saying to me…even in English."

"Tom!" Courtney was about to admonish him when the woman walked away, muttering about what an asshole she'd been assigned to. Courtney bit her lip to keep from laughing out loud.

"What?"

"The woman's delightful. She certainly went out of her way last night and this morning to help me settle in. The house is immaculate and the food smells divine." Her mouth watered as she looked at the pile of buttermilk pancakes, sausage and fresh fruit. "You're lucky to have someone like her. You don't know how hard it is to get good help with the summer coming soon."

Tom took a sip of his coffee and cut into his triple stack. "Aunt Elizabeth insisted I hire her. Seems she got laid off from a great job when the President sacked his chief of staff and the family moved back to Chicago. They didn't want to take any of their employees with them. So Auntie told me I'd be a fool not to 'snatch her up.' I've gotta admit that I've been pretty fortunate in hiring people to work. Guess it's the recession."

Tongue in cheek, she replied, "I imagine this place takes quite a few people to keep it up. With summer coming, there will be even more to do." Courtney swallowed her food and took a sip of tea, thankful their conversation had gone well so far.

The two ate, making idle conversation about the article in the paper over the next fifteen minutes. Tom caught Courtney up on the goings-on in the family, laughing at the antics of his niece, Lizzie Clinton, Kate's daughter. Kate was the youngest Hallock sibling. Courtney knew she'd left the area and her job as CEO of the farm several years ago to marry the love of her life. She was surprised Tom hadn't brought up the embezzlement case once. But, as the Director often said, "The proverbial shoe was about to drop."

And drop it did.

"Natasha," Tom called out to the housekeeper, "I think we're done here."

Courtney looked at her half-eaten plate. "I'm not done. What's going on?"

"You're done. You can get a snack from the Hampton Coffee Company when we get to the office. Or there's a bistro that's opening up by the hardware store."

"But - " The man leveled a determined look her way. He had an agenda. She was apparently a part of it, whether she wanted to be or not. Well, there would never be a better time to inform him of hers.

Tom stood. "Grab your tea. We'll go into my study."

She looked at Natasha, who merely nodded, an assurance the house was wired for her friend to come to her aid, if need be.

Courtney followed Tom as he made his way out of the kitchen and to the office. Oh, crap. Sarah! She hadn't texted her. She should have made the call the minute she hung up on Rick. Well, she'd make an excuse when this so-called talk was over, before they headed out to his office, and get a message sent.

She followed him into a dark-paneled room that was out of character with the rest of the décor of the home and sat in a club chair while he walked behind his desk. She placed her mug of tea on his desktop.

When he leaned back in his chair, his eyes pierced hers. "You, Courtney Stockton, do not work for the FBI."

She had all she could do not to react. "I most certainly do. For your information, I'm using vacation time to help Rick with your case."

"I saw those blue suits and pumps and white shirts in the closet at the safe house. There's only one company that has their agents dress like that. Don't tell me you don't know who I'm referring to."

Think fast. Courtney leaned forward in her chair. "Just what were you doing, looking through that closet?" Tom leaned closer and placed his elbows on his desk, his eyes scanning her face for a reaction. He wasn't going to get one. She pointed at him with her forefinger. "You had no business checking out my work clothes. The Bureau has me on an assignment where I'm doing office work. I'm not out on the street, Tom. I couldn't take the stress after what I went through with that international company I worked for. The last job in London almost killed me, literally. When I came back to New York, I did a few minor consulting jobs for Rick. One overlapped with the FBI. They liked my work. I was ready to do something full-time with my background so they put me on their payroll. Why would you think otherwise?"

"Those suits are standard issue dress code for the CIA. There isn't a day Aunt Elizabeth doesn't dress like that."

"The CIA!" Courtney chortled. "Tom, I needed a job with *less* stress. A desk job, not one that would have me globetrotting all over again."

"Well, I don't believe you, since your passport says otherwise.

And what's with your memory box in the bottom of that closet?"

Take a deep breath. You need to get him off this topic. He's sniffing like a dog into matters that could get him killed.

"You looked at my passport? And what were you doing looking at my box?"

"The passport was hidden under the clothes in the dresser. You've been all over Europe. Hit every big city on the globe."

"That's for my old job." Courtney's stomach twisted into a knot. "Did you look in that box?"

"No, I was about to, but Joe came looking for me. Why?"

"Thank God. It's locked for a very good reason. Have you any idea why?"

Tom shook his head.

"It's where I keep my gun."

Tom's eyes widened.

Feeling as if the floor was going to give way under her feet at any moment, Courtney desperately needed to relay the plan for him to aid in her cover.

"Since you've decided you're so interested in my life, let's talk about my need for a better cover. Coming with Rick to your office and meeting Jim and the STPD was, in retrospect, not such a great idea. I'm going to need better access to *your* inner circle. Rick shared with me he has some reservations regarding several of the people working the investigation."

Tom leaned back, a puzzled look on his face. "I don't follow."

Courtney leaned back in her seat, her hands gripping its armrest for support. "People know I've come back home because I gave up that job in London. Only a few know I live with Rick in New York, but out of those, several know I work for the FBI. Rick didn't want to share with anyone else that I'm in your house as a bodyguard. But I need a more personal cover, one that will give me unlimited access."

"I have a feeling I'm not going to like this." Tom rose and she did as well. "Walk with me. I have to talk to Natasha about dinner tonight."

As they walked down the hallway, Courtney put her arm through his and felt him tense at the contact.

"So, in as few words as possible, what's the plan?" He tried to disengage his arm, but she hung on tight.

"We're getting engaged."

Suddenly, a loud crash of dishes came from the kitchen.

As Tom turned toward her, she glanced up to see the look on his face. She fully expected the man to explode, yank away from her, or tell her she was crazy. Instead, there was a smile on his face a mile wide. She shook her head, not believing his reaction.

"I like the sound of it." Tom was actually nodding in agreement!

Courtney, still shocked by the expression of joy on the man's face, said, "The sound of what?"

"Courtney Stockton Hallock. It has a nice ring to it, don't you think? Boy, I can't wait until Mother gets wind of this. She's going to be thrilled!"

CHAPTER FIFTEEN

Hailey and her staff worked diligently since daybreak, bringing order to the facility's conference room for Rick's upcoming meeting. She'd taken orders for coffee, tea and Danish, which were delivered a few minutes earlier from the Hampton Coffee Shop. Rick, Jim, Hailey, several members of the staff, the CEO, Courtney and Tom had assembled around the long rectangular wooden table. The task at hand, to go over the latest updates of the B&E and put into place plans for the next few days.

In a blue pinstriped suit, Jack Jessop sat at the head of the table. "So, let me make sure I understand what you've just told me. Our *entire* system was compromised…hacked. And the company has been vulnerable for three weeks. Have I got that right?"

Rick shook his head in the affirmative. "As we informed Tom, my team uncovered an encrypted code embedded in your new software. It allows, when activated, someone outside, or within," Tom watched as his friend's eyes fell on Hailey and the two staff members, "to take control of the movement of the monies in and out of your accounts. Also, whoever it is can easily take control of your computers at any time. My team thinks that's exactly what happened yesterday during Hailey's training session."

Knowing Tom had been briefed by Courtney, he still had a few remaining questions left on his mind. "Hailey, care to weigh in with anything? Our backgrounds overlap. This could only be possible if passwords were shared. Or someone wrote new code to input the stats into the databases' spreadsheets."

He glanced across the table at Courtney, who seemed to assess each of the room's occupants while taking copious notes on a yellow legal pad. So far, she'd filled up four pages by his count.

Hailey, normally professionally attired, her hair perfectly coiffed, looked weary. Today, she was dressed in work clothes, her shirt-sleeves rolled up to her elbows. "I'm as shocked as you. I figured since there'd been a problem with the power over the last couple of days, the outage yesterday was from LILCO working down the street at the new restaurant. When the computers stayed down, I thought, why waste time. I sent everyone out for an extended early lunch break, myself included. I came back to find a crime scene, police cars with lights flashing and you all gathered inside trying to make sense of the trashed office." It seemed as if she was about to cry again. Tom had had enough of her tears yesterday. She pointed to the Chief of Police. "Chief Benjamin said to put the office back together as best we could."

Rick leaned across the table as if ready to pounce. "And have you found anything missing now that you've had time to look things over? Anything seem out of the ordinary?"

Hailey's body language turned defiant. The woman had been under the gun since yesterday afternoon, but Tom had no sympathy for her. "*No*, Mr. Stockton. To me, it just looked as if someone came in and decided to turn everything inside-out and upside-down. The file drawer in Mr. Jessop's office was definitely rifled. The private drawer to Mr. Hallock's desk was jimmied open. I've no idea what he keeps in there. If there was anything important, it's gone."

"Tom?" Rick asked, turning to look at him. "You didn't share this with us yesterday."

His hands rose to ward off more interrogation. This was about the office, not him. "Nobody allowed me time to check things out. We weren't here long enough. You two," he pointed to Rick and Jim, "whisked me out of here and sent me home with Courtney. You told me I'd come back today when CSU was finished and Hailey's staff had put the office back together."

"Exactly what did you have in that drawer, sir?" Jim had taken out his small notepad.

Gauging the disgruntled look Rick shot his way, Tom chose his words carefully. "The drawer had some old invoices, a few blank thumb drives and a list of passwords." Which were planted and are of no use to anybody, Thomas thought silently to himself. Somebody probably thinks they've discovered a gold mine. Won't they be surprised when they find out otherwise?

Jim pointed at both Tom and Hailey. "Are you telling me the access codes to your accounts aren't locked up in a safe or put in a safe deposit box?"

"To be honest, Chief," Tom replied, "Hailey's new on the scene, but is taking the business into the twenty-first century. I had paper copies of everything until she changed the system." *And I still do. People just don't know where I've stored them.*

"Well, someone accessed them," Rick replied. "It's important we know what you do have in your possession today. You and your staff are not going to be able to be given the right to use some of the accounts. As of early this morning, the Board of Directors transferred the unhacked assets in Hallock Farm's possession into other funds. Those will be monitored by an independent party until we can get to the bottom of this scam."

Tom noticed Hailey stiffen. Did the woman have something to hide? He always had a problem believing she really divorced herself from her brother and his lifestyle as she'd insisted. He made a mental note to ask Rick and Courtney their own take on his CPA.

"Are we finished?" Hailey asked. "My staff really has a lot more work to do if we're going to open in two days. The phone is ringing off the hook. We have a lot of damage control to do, as well."

"I think we've covered everything." Jim Benjamin rose. Hailey and her staff followed suit.

"Sit!" Rick commanded. "There's one more thing to get out of the way."

Puzzled, Tom looked at his friend and also took in the fact that Courtney did not seem flustered in the least. He wished he could see what she'd been writing on the paper in front of her as the meeting progressed.

"Jim, this report," Rick flicked his fingers at the pile of papers sitting on the table, "did *not* report the security cameras were *not* working. What have you got to say about the deletion of an important piece of evidence?"

Tom's head snapped up. He took a good look at the man who sat opposite the CEO. The feeling that nothing had been accomplished in the last forty-five minutes set his teeth on edge. Now that he'd given it some thought, Jim seemed a bit smug during the entire meeting.

Jim's eyes darted to every corner of the room, avoiding contact with Rick's. The man was clearly flustered by Rick's boldness and public tongue-lashing.

"I…ah…" Jim's words tripped over his tongue. "I dictated my report on my phone and sent it to our secretary to type up. That fact should have been included, Rick. I swear when I get back to the office, I'll have it all straightened out."

"You do that."

For some uncanny reason, Tom sensed his friend didn't believe a word spewed out of Jim's mouth.

What was going on? He was glad he wasn't sitting in Rick's chair. If looks could kill, Rick would be a dead man from the glare Jim sent his way. The atmosphere in the room was going downhill fast. Tension mounted. Tom had had enough for the time being and wanted out. But he'd arrived wanting answers. And he knew just who was going to give them to him…if he treated her right.

* * *

Thomas had been caught daydreaming several times during the meeting. He thought about Courtney's plan to better her cover and his immediate reaction. He was surprised at how he'd acted in the moment. He couldn't help but be happy that out of something awful, the possibility of going bankrupt, had come something so totally unexpected. The woman who'd left without so much as a "good-bye" had returned in the blink of an eye, more beautiful and stunning than ever. Yes, Courtney had a job to do, sorting out the sordid affairs of the embezzlement. That was by day, wasn't it? With any luck, she'd be his at night. Thomas couldn't help but dream of the perfect ways to fill the time they'd be together.

Before leaving the office, Rick had given him specific instructions, out of the earshot of the others, to report early the next morning to the Stockton home in Hampton Beach. Outside, he and Courtney got in the Town Car for the short ride home to Gin Lane.

For the first few minutes, the two traveled in silence.

Courtney spoke first. "We need to talk about last night, Thomas."

Tom looked over to see her gazing out the window, the scenery of hedgerow after hedgerow whizzing by. "I take it you weren't ready for my reaction to your supposed cover."

She turned to look at him, her dark eyes locked onto his. "We're not playing 'house.' This is serious. Hallock Farm is nearing financial ruin. Don't make this a game…especially out of us."

Thomas smiled. "You're the one who proposed. I simply said 'Yes.'"

Courtney had placed both hands in her lap. Sitting so close, it was easy to reach over and grab hold of her right hand. She tried to snatch it away, but he held on tight and wouldn't let go. She sighed, as if in defeat, letting him have his way. He was surprised at how rough her hand was. Turning it palm side up, he looked down and ushered a swift outtake of air. A large scar ran from the base of her palm to the tip of her forefinger.

"What happened here? Don't tell me you got this doing a desk job?"

She shrugged. "It's part of the reason I left Europe. Leave it at that." She tried again to yank her hand from he wouldn't let go.

Thomas raised her injured palm to his lips, placing light kisses along the scar.

"Please, don't, Tom." She nodded toward the front of the car. He ignored her.

The car drew to a stop in front of the main entrance of his estate. Dusk had fallen. There was a definite chill in the air. Thomas released Courtney's hand when the door opened. He slid out, but this time waited for her to follow. She exited the car, her laptop bag slung over her shoulder, and stopped. He realized she was waiting for his cue to enter the house.

"*Mi casa es su casa, mi querida,*" he whispered in her ear as he took her arm and tucked it through his. When Courtney didn't argue, he knew she was playing her role. He'd informed Natasha last night he and Ms. Stockton had become engaged, but asked she keep the details a secret until the news could be shared with his family. Natasha had flown into a rapid litany in Russian of what he hoped were good wishes by kissing him and Courtney on both cheeks.

Walking in the front door with Courtney on his arm was living his dream. He stopped, hearing a gasp come from his right side. Apparently, she was just as surprised as he was by the sight that awaited them. The lights had been dimmed. Lit candles were strategically placed around the foyer. He and Courtney looked at each other in awe and moved slowly toward the kitchen, taking in the ambiance of their surroundings.

"Natasha!" he called out, but there was no reply. Reaching the eating nook, he spied a note on the round table. He opened the card and attempted to read the elegant handwriting.

Judas Priest! Why did I hire the woman? The damn note's in Russian!

"What's the matter? Has something happened?" Courtney laid her bag on the island and came to stand by his side.

"It's my idiot housekeeper. Apparently she's set the mood for us, but she's left me a note in Russian. She knows I don't speak a word of it. How the hell are we suppose to figure out what's for dinner?"

He spied Courtney's body relax. "Give me that." She grabbed the note out of his hand.

"You're a numbers girl like me, Court. Russian's not your thing."

"Well, hotshot. Just for your information, I may have majored in forensic accounting at George Washington, but I minored in linguistics. I speak *five*," she held up five fingers on her left hand, practically in his face to make her point, "languages. Russian being the one I'm most fluent in."

"Well then, hotshot, what does's it say? I'm starving."

He watched Courtney read the note once, then twice. The second time *she* was speaking in Russian. And she didn't seem happy.

"Translation, Court? We don't have all night." Tom had an idea for how he wanted to spend the evening and wanted dinner out of the way as soon as possible.

Courtney looked down at the note and read, "Dinner's been warming in the oven. The formal dining room is set up. All we have to do is eat and leave the dishes in the sink. She'll clean them up in the morning…and…"She crinkled up the paper and tossed it on the table, again muttering in the foreign tongue. Thomas didn't understand what had riled her up. There was more in that note than she was letting on.

"And? You don't seem happy. What else should I know about? Has she quit?"

"No. It says she's gone to stay in the village with a friend for the night… so we can have some privacy."

Thomas grinned broadly. "I *knew* Aunt Elizabeth wouldn't steer me wrong when I hired that woman." He reached out for his "bride-to-be" but she ducked under his arm and headed for the oven on the other side of the kitchen.

"Like you said, Tom. I'm starving, too. What ever you have planned for tonight is going to have to wait. I'll grab the casserole. You pick out the wine and bring that bread in the basket over there." She pointed to a basket with a napkin strategically placed over the top. Courtney, with potholders holding up both ends of the hot dish, whizzed by him in the direction of the dining room.

"Holy crap!" he heard Courtney shout out. Grabbing hold of the wine and the basket, he hustled down the short hallway, coming up sort at the entrance to the dining room.

Natasha had been a mind reader. He could not have asked for a more romantic setting. The table had been laid with his mother's best lace tablecloth. The decorator's choice of china and Waterford crystal glasses were out of the boxes where they'd been stored for ages in the garage, along with the sterling place settings. A dozen red roses stood tall as the table's centerpiece.

Walking up to stand adjacent to Courtney, he saw her taking it all in. She'd put the casserole down on an extremely decorative hotplate. She started to circle the intimate setting, touching everything, the tablecloth, the linens, the china, the glassware.

"This is beautiful…stunning. We might think the woman's a bit misdirected, Tom, but you have to admit her heart's in the right place."

To Thomas, it seemed by the expression on Courtney's face, she was seeing an occasion like this for the first time. Her tone was wistful. She sounded as if there had been very few moments like this in her life. Was there someone special now? He found himself growing jealous at the mere thought.

Courtney gazed up, trying to mask her dark smoldering eyes. He, too, felt the pull, the power of the festive room.

He cleared his throat. "I can see where she planned on us to sit." He motioned to the end of the table. Two place settings had been set, allowing a couple to chat intimately. "Dinner is served, my lady." He bowed and offered Courtney his arm. It broke the ice.

Courtney sighed then chuckled. "Come on. Even you have to say this is really quite spectacular. I think you should give Natasha a raise."

I'd pay the woman a million dollars if it would keep you in my life.

Thomas pulled out her chair and she sat, drawing the linen napkin into her lap. He followed suit, placing one in his. "Smells divine. No?"

Much to Thomas's dismay, little talking occurred as they

dined.

While he finished his meal, he thought of the hidden treasure he'd found in Natasha's ability to cook. He'd have to introduce her to Hannah, the Hallocks' housekeeper of forty years. It would be ideal if she could make several of the infamous Irish dishes he loved so much.

Thomas realized his mind had wandered. Turning to say something to Courtney, he saw he was alone. While his thoughts had roamed elsewhere, the plates had been cleared. He rose and went in search of his "date," finding her at the kitchen sink, rinsing the dishes and placing them off to the side in the sink.

"What are you doing? That's why I've got a housekeeper." Thomas was curt, but he had other things he wanted to discuss.

"Just getting the food off, so it's not hard to clean up in the morning. It really wouldn't take me a minute to load all this in the dishwasher, but I don't think the china and crystal can go in." Again, that wistful longing rang out in her tone.

Thomas stepped around the island and for a brief moment, massaged her shoulders. She immediately stiffened. Turning her to face him, he tipped her chin up.

"What do you think you're doing?" She tried to back up, but the counter stopped her retreat.

"I'm going to kiss you." He touched his finger to her lips.

"No, Tom. Don't. We can't... You can't. My job..."

Thomas silenced her by brushing his lips lightly over hers. A swift intake of breath rustled in his ears, and he knew it didn't come from him. Wrapping his arms around her waist, he drew her to him once more, bent his head and repeated the light kiss. He expected her to fight him off. However, she responded as if she'd been in the desert with no water for days.

He grabbed her by her arms, pushing her back ever so slightly so he could look into her eyes. He had to ask. He had to know.

"What's the matter?" Courtney asked. "You're looking at me strange."

"Why did you leave me, Court? Why did you run and stay away? How could you do that after the night we spent together?"

The color drained from her face, and a mask dropped, as if she was devoid of any emotions. She stabbed her forefinger so hard into his chest it actually hurt. "Don't you lay the blame on me, Thomas Hallock! It was all you! *You* didn't want *me!*" Her voice choked up as she stepped around him. In a flash, she bolted toward the back staircase that led up to her wing of the house.

He stood rooted in place, stunned by her remarks. Thomas listened to the pounding of her footsteps as she made her way to her room. He flinched at the bang of a door slamming shut, the sound echoing to all parts of the house.

Running his fingers through his hair in frustration, he tried to fathom how things had gone so very wrong so fast. He'd been an idiot by acting too quickly with his feelings. The cards were stacked against him. By the look in her eyes, he'd crossed the line. But what had she meant? He hadn't wanted her?

Those thoughts were for another time. Deciding to climb the stairs, he placed his foot on the first step and stopped. He ran his fingers over his lips, the memory of her warm mouth on his. Yes, she was here to do her job, but was it possible to resurrect their past?

The moment she and Rick found the missing clues that solved the equation of the embezzlement scam, he'd make his move. Courtney Stockton was *not* leaving his life ever again!

CHAPTER SIXTEEN

Courtney lay on the bed, tears dripping from her eyes onto the pillowcase. She couldn't believe, after all the years that had passed, she had any tears left to give.

Someone pounding on the door had her sitting straight up in bed. Had something happened? Tash would have already entered, and Rick would have called. No, it could only be one person. And the last she wanted to face at the moment.

"Court! Court! Open up. I'm sorry. I was a shit. We have to talk."

She had no interest in carrying on a conversation regarding the night in question. Now, she was not just physically spent, but due to Thomas's persistence, she was emotionally drained, as well. And she had a long night ahead of her.

"Go away!" Her hands clutched at the quilt on the bed to keep herself from throwing a jar full of seashells from the bedside table. Why did she feel blindsided? She knew the subject would come up at some point. "Just go. I can't talk right now."

His soft voice came through the closed door. "We have to clear the air. Don't tell me you haven't thought how our history could affect your proposal. There can't be any secrets if people are really going to believe we've become engaged."

Did he think she hadn't been weighted down when considering how their history could possibly come in the way of her cover? God, she'd had time to mull over every memory: every kiss, caress, lick and orgasm of that night.

Now all he was doing was making her angry. She had things to do, and he'd gone and stuck emotion into her objectivity. Damn him!

"Go back to your study and have a Scotch. Leave me alone!"

A hand slapped the door. "Have it your way for now. But we're not done. You're going to tell me why you ran. We have to work together and if you want me to play my role, I've got to know."

Was the man not listening when she'd stormed out of the kitchen? Had he truly forgotten all he'd said that morning? Hearing the sound of his footsteps walking away from her door, she breathed a sigh of relief and relaxed back on the bed. Maybe Rick was right, and her plan hadn't been a good idea after all.Knowing she had to meet Sarah Adams at eleven o'clock, she set the alarm on her phone. Plumping up her pillow, she snuggled under the quilt and closed her eyes. It took only minutes before she'd drifted off into a troubled sleep.

CHAPTER SEVENTEEN

Fox Hollow Inn
North Fork

"'Tis been a long time, lass." Reggie Litchfield released his bear-hug, vise-like grip on Courtney. His wife, Victoria, stood by his side, motherly tears of joy streaming down her face. Her history with Reggie and Victoria Litchfield went way back.

"It's been a while." Their welcome warmed her. She placed her laptop bag on the round kitchen table and turned to look at them. Oh, how they'd aged. "When was the last time I saw you?"

"Seven years ago in Paris." Victoria spoke, her Scottish accent not as thick as her husband's. "The last place Elizabeth sent us before we filed our retirement papers."

Courtney watched Reggie lovingly place his arm around his wife's shoulders. The two were quite a pair, and the three of them had had quite an adventure, if one could actually classify a mission in such a way. She owed them her life, literally.

"So, now you've settled here. Nice operation you've got here – a bed and breakfast *plus* a marina." Courtney took in the homey feel of her surroundings. The aroma of freshly baked chocolate chip scones wafted through the air. "Suits you both. Too bad we're not here under more pleasant circumstances."

"Court, the clock is ticking. It's late." Rick tapped his watch. He'd been edgy since he picked her up in Southampton. She'd been late. Thomas hadn't gone back to his study as planned and stood out on the deck by the kitchen over an hour past the time she'd napped and wanted to leave.

The back door squeaked as someone entered. Knowing who would walk through the door, Courtney still reacted by reaching for her gun. She pushed Rick behind her to shield him. Upon seeing Sarah Adams enter, her hands raised above her head, Courtney let out a sigh of relief and released her hand from her weapon.

"Finally! What the hell took so long?" Rick needed to tone down his impatience, or he'd find an adversary in the girl who walked in the door. He'd actually heard bits and bits of unclassified information that the two had undertaken in the past, but had never met the woman. From experience, Courtney wanted to tell him not to piss her off.

"Easy, lad." Reggie attempted to assuage him. "Sarah has a good reason for being a bit behind." He eyed the new arrival. "What say you, lassie?"

Sarah walked farther into the room. "Things are going down over at base camp, Court. One of your brother's team came incognito to the club to 'become a member.' Left me their latest findings. I've got them with me. Andrew said to deactivate our GPS chips in our phones immediately."

Everyone rushed to do as instructed. Done, her brother placed his on the table. Courtney had put two and two together and knew that part of the meeting had something to do with a message he'd received several days earlier, but no matter how hard she'd tried to get him to open up, he clammed up and said only "certain parties" would be privy to the information tonight.

Rick cocked his head to one side. "Wait. What about my car? It's equipped with all the latest navigational tools."

"Taken care of." Sarah held up a large blue chip for all to see.

He stared at Sarah, dumbfounded. Courtney couldn't help but giggle. *Sarah thinks of everything. Always two steps ahead.*

The lion was about to roar. "You took my—"

Courtney placed a hand on his arm, and he stopped midsentence.

"Listen, Einstein. It's just a chip. You're safe, and I'm a pro. I promise you'll be good to go when you need to. Now, are we getting down to business or what? *You're* the one who demanded I be in on this." Hands on her hips, Sarah stared Rick down as he made for the kitchen table.

Victoria, in an attempt to ease the tension in her soft Scottish brogue, spoke up. "I've got freshly brewed coffee and tea. Scones, too. Settle yourselves around the table. Rick is right. Let's get to work."

As Courtney sat beside her brother, Sarah pointed directly at her and added, "And *you*, my lady, have big problems. Mrs. H knows you're back in town *and,* do I hear a drum roll? That you're staying at Thomas's house! Eckart's was closed for breakfast this morning so Matt and I stopped in for coffee and bagels at the estate. Mrs. H cornered me in the kitchen while we were grabbing a bite to eat. I pled the fifth. I swear. I really did. But Hannah informed me, when we were about to take off, there's a huge family dinner in the not-so-distant future. You know where *that* might lead." Sarah winked and grinned from ear to ear.

Smart ass. I want to slap that prissy grin right off her face. If I didn't like her so much, I would. She's relishing in my discomfort over this ordeal.

Finished giving Courtney and the others the happenings at the main estate, Sarah plopped herself in the chair next to Rick. *Have mercy on all of us. Please don't let her get him riled up.*

As Victoria poured coffee and tea for the group and passed out plates for the scones, she said, "Rick, tell us what's so important."

Rick nodded, and as everyone helped themselves to drinks and scones, he picked up his phone from the table. "You guys have to see these three texts Janie Walker sent me right before she was murdered."

Courtney's head snapped around. "Texts? Why didn't you bring this up before? Did you get them while we were in—?"

"Because we've been in mixed company too long," Rick cut in. "There are a few people in my supposed inner circle I don't quite trust...yet."

Courtney gripped the edge of the table. "Who? Have I been in contact with them? Did I say something I shouldn't?"

"Stop already!" Rick glared at her. They'd never get anything accomplished at this rate if she and Rick did nothing but badger each other back and forth.

"Sarah, can I have those documents you got from my IT guy?"

From within her jacket, Sarah withdrew a large folder and passed it to Rick. She said nothing. Courtney could read her face. She, too, was waiting. He opened it, drew out several color-coded papers and began to read slowly. The silence in the room was deafening.

Reggie drummed his fingers on the table. Victoria hummed some Scottish tune, and Courtney wanted to slap her brother upside his head if he didn't share the intel soon. He'd been about to divulge the contents of the texts when he'd skirted off onto the topic of the papers. Texts from a dead girl. That had been a shocker. Why on earth would he keep the messages from her, of all people? Rick was playing things extremely close to the vest. So unlike his usual demeanor of delegating tasks to his team and letting them get the details.

"Einstein? You made a big deal out of my being here." It was evident Sarah's patience was wearing thin. "I don't have all night. Certain people are awaiting a briefing ASAP. Would you mind hurrying up? Give."

Courtney could tell Sarah was used to ASAP answers and a protocol that worked precisely by the clock. She wouldn't doubt the woman was the conduit to the Director and Sam, and even Joe. Quite frankly, she shared the woman's frustration.

Rick finally broke his silence. "Sorry. I had to figure out the best chronological way to lay out the facts. I'm at a loss. I'm in need of all of you to put the puzzle together." He opened the screen of his phone and scrolled down to Janie's messages.

"Her TOD was estimated to be about midnight the night we were at the Red Lion. Two days before she died, she sent this." He read: "'JR @ HCC w/ HAILEY.'"

"JR?" Sarah asked. "Initials for whom?"

Rick replied, "Jason Rockwell. A pompous ass with lots of 'legal' money, buying up real estate. Jim told me the guy's trying to show a legit side to his import/export business based in the Bronx. He's supposedly turned over a new leaf. But his rap sheet is a mile long with a twelve year stint in prison for extortion and attempted murder. It's believed someone still ran his operation from the outside."

"But, Hailey was vetted and passed her background check," Courtney stated. "The Director used every resource she could use and gave her approval. Hailey was adamant she had no ties with her brother since he came out of prison."

Rick scrolled up to the next message and glanced over at her. "Apparently, all is not what it seems, Court."

"So she lied when she said she was no longer in touch with

her brother."

Sarah snorted. "Ya think?"

"Why the hell would she even think it was wise to be seen at the Hampton Coffee Company, a very public place?" Courtney took out her laptop and started to take notes of the texts and thoughts at the meeting.

"I'll dig around," Sarah said. "See if he's trying to infiltrate the Hallock inner social circle, now that his sister's an employee. There's a gala in a few weeks at the country club. I can't fathom he'd even think of going, but it is a charity event."

Rick, after watching the woman next to him, turned back to his phone. "This second text was sent the morning she was killed: 'STPD AND HBPD watching.'"

Courtney was too stunned to speak, but Sarah voiced the same thoughts. "Janie had a deal with the DA's office? Correct?"

"That's why Jim and I were using her and Sammy to find out what was possibly leaking out in town about Tom's business. Tongues wag all the time. It's like a one-up-you club." Rick arranged the papers in some semblance of order in the middle of the table.

Reggie got up and came to stand at his shoulder. "Finish up, lad. You know I like to think on my feet. I've got an idea brewin'."

"Maybe she was telling you someone was eyeing her from inside the department," Sarah countered. "You told Courtney you hadn't shared these publicly as you've had a few doubts regarding people you've been working with. You've been entrenched with both police departments from the top down. Could she have tried to warn you there was a mole in the circle of the law enforcement community?"

Courtney's train of thoughts paralleled Sarah's to a "t". "What did the last one say, RIck?"

Rick brought it up on the screen. "'MAIN BEACH

MASTER KEY.'"

"Isn't Main Beach just a public access road to get over the dunes in Easthampton?" Courtney remarked. "I don't remember it very well."

"Main Beach was completely redone several years ago," Sarah said. "There are lockers now and cabanas, much like at the Sunfish. Maybe a master key was stashed in one of the lockers for pick up. But for what? Tom's office, his house? A safety deposit box?"

"All I know is," Rick said, "I've got to piece these together with the B&E." He stood up. Reggie was leaning over Courtney's shoulder, studying the print-outs. "Looks like I need to approach Jim regarding Hailey. She's lied. Yes, there might be a mole. If it's true, I'm way to skeptical to share that with him. She must have found out something someone didn't want her to know if she was being trailed around town. And she wound up dead. The team's one hundred percent positive the break-in was done so our perps could buy time to get onto the Cloud. Once Hailey returned, she'd be up and running into the farm's accounts with the new passwords she'd received to start transferring more monies. What she doesn't know is it gave Andrew and Troy the time they needed to falsify the passwords so that they can now track the system's usage. With the 'real' money left, they can follow the trail."

Courtney sat back in her chair, her head swimming with possible scenarios. She looked at Sarah, whose brow furrowed. She could practically see the mental checklist being tallied within the woman's mind. Funny how much alike they were. She'd been doing the exact same thing as Rick talked on about the case laying out the facts to Reggie and Victoria.

Sarah finally stood up and stretched, walking once around the room. Joining Rick and Reggie, she asked, "Who's got a pen?"

"Here." Rick pulled one from his pocket.

Sarah leaned over the table and read through the three texts and the messages for herself. "Court, remember when I was in London and I called you about the cryptic messages I'd been receiving and the map that mysteriously was slipped under my apartment door?"

Courtney's eyes widened. "Are you thinking maybe the same have occurred here? Or something similar?" Courtney looked up at the Scotsman. "Reggie, have you got that tourist map of the streets of Southampton?"

"Sure do." He walked over and rummaged through a pile of phonebooks and atlases, pulling a laminated map out of the pile. He came back and placed it on the table, moving the phone and the messages to the side.

With map in hand, Courtney pushed the men to the side so they could watch as she and Sarah went to work. Taking the messages, which contained the GPS tracking of all the calls on Janie's cell that were placed from three days before until the last, in tandem, the women marked off Janie's trail.

"What are you doing?" Rick was so close he practically breathed in her ear.

"Patience. We're tracking Janie's movements from the GPS in her phone. Andrew must have realized there was not only a pattern to the money transfers, but came up with idea of looking to see what he'd glean from her cell phone records. She used her street smarts, Rick. Janie left you a trail of breadcrumbs! When she texted or called, it pinged a location off a cell tower. That had to be why she didn't dare get in touch with you face-to-face. She knew what would happen if she texted. But whoever killed her wasn't thinking. Sloppy."

"What do you mean, gel?" asked Reggie.

"A pro would have destroyed her phone the minute they took her. I can see where they nabbed her."

"I don't see anything." She glanced over her shoulder to the curious look on Rick's face.

Reggie patted Courtney on her shoulder. "Good work, lassies. Only an operative can see it. Mark it off. Victoria, get a marker. That pen's not going to work on that laminated surface."

Minutes, later, permanent marker in hand, with Sarah by her side rereading the messages with locations, Courtney marked the map. When done, she connected the dots. For someone with little to no law enforcement experience, Janie weaved up and down the streets of the village, walking the main street and alleys, placing phone calls and texts.

All five people circled the table, stared down at the finished product, and collectively gasped. By connecting the dotted lines, the word BOMB was clearly spelled out. A dotted line led out of town heading in the direction of Thomas's house, but stopped at the intersection of Main Street and Jobs Lane. An "X" marked the spot where his house now stood.

"Holy mother of God!" Rick shouted as Reggie and Victoria made the sign of the cross on their chests. Courtney began to hyperventilate, which set into motion a bevy of activity to keep her from passing out. Sarah was at her side, placing a chair beneath her legs. Victoria held an ice-cold dishtowel to the back of her neck.

"Rick?" She could barely speak. She felt as if the bit of coffee and scones were going to vacate her stomach.

"Easy, girl. We're going to get these SOBs. I've got to get back to base camp. You know what you need to do with Thomas. Keep him secluded and guarded as much as you can. You can do this."

"And you—" Rick spun around only to bump into Sarah.

"I know my job. Call Joe. Get the final directions from the Director. Report back. You going to be okay, Court?"

She attempted to stand, but Reggie's hand on her shoulder held her firmly in her seat. "Stay seated and get your thoughts together. We've been in circumstances far worse than this. Remember, you're highly trained. You'll make the right decisions."

"You're right, Reggie. The girl didn't leave us any timeframe so every minute counts. She must have been killed before she was able to." Her voice still shook, but she felt herself regaining her former strength. Her knees no longer felt like rubber.

Rick was on his feet, making his way to the door, shouting out orders. "We move on this *now*. Other than our own agents, we work and tell *no one* else. Have I made that clear?"

The four nodded in agreement. Within minutes, Rick, Sarah and Courtney exited the house and headed to their respective destinations.

Courtney closed her eyes and prayed silently as Rick hastily drove through the dark back roads home to Southampton.

God, it's me, Courtney. Please give me one more chance to tell Tom how much I've loved him. Don't deprive me of the opportunity of seeing if he can forgive my stupidity and stubbornness all those years ago and love me back.

CHAPTER EIGHTEEN

Shinnecock Inlet
Dune Road

The black Town Car drove into the parking lot overlooking the Shinnecock Inlet's outlet to the Atlantic Ocean. At that time of night, one couldn't see the splendor of the entrance to the bay, a place where a multitude of fishing vessels came into dock and sell their wares. Besides, it was eerily dark. No moon, just black storm clouds rolling in from the south. The ocean roared as the storm moved closer to shore, and the rain pattered lightly on the windshield. High tide was coming in so Jason's meeting had to be quick. Flooding occurred rapidly on Dune Road in that area, and right now, it was the last thing he needed to deal with.

After about fifteen minutes, his driver spoke up. "Boss. His car just went behind the Bar & Grill."

"Drive me over. Let me off. Then drive once over Ponquogue Bridge, turn around, and come back for me. I told him I'd give him twenty minutes. No more, no less."

"I don't want to leave you alone with him. That guy makes even me nervous. You got your gun?"

Jason reached into his pocket and patted the pistol. "Yeah. I'll use it if I have to but let's hope it won't come to that. He's still too valuable to me. Move out."

The driver put the car in reverse and turned around in the parking lot. As they drove slowly around the Shinnecock Bar & Grill to its rear entrance, Jason saw the brown car hidden behind a large stack of wood.

"Let me out by his passenger door."

The Town Car came to a stop. Jason pulled his raincoat's hood up over his head and stepped out onto the gravel. He waved his driver off and opened the door of the unmarked police car, hopping in next to the driver in the front seat.

Jason growled at him from where he sat behind the steering wheel. "Finally, a private place to meet. You're getting the idea. This better be good. It's late, and the bridge is going to close at midnight with the storm heading in."

"Here." Jim Benjamin offered him a cup of hot coffee. "I know you take it with cream."

Jason took the cup with his left hand and placed it in the cup holder, his hand still wrapped around the pistol in his right pocket. Until he knew the man with him didn't have a hidden agenda, other than to impart some crucial information, he wasn't touching what might be tainted coffee. He'd worked in the "business" too long.

"Come on. I can give you..." He looked down at his florescent-faced watch. "...seventeen minutes. What's got you so hell fired up we had to meet?"

"Stockton had a meeting tonight with his sister. Something's not right. I'm being kept out of the loop. He knows something. I think it's got to do with Janie Walker."

Jason's pulse galloped. If he didn't need more from the man, he'd have pulled the gun out of his pocket and ended their relationship right then and there. But he sensed there was more that needed to be said. And, he wasn't going to like the news.

Had he not projected this very thing would happen, but was told everything was "under control" and not to worry?

"You obviously sent someone to tail them. Where'd they meet? Did the man get close enough to hear their conversation?"

"Ah…that's the first problem." Jim's voice wavered. Apparently, he'd lost the tough guy persona since their visit at Main Beach, Jason thought.

First? There's more than *one?* Out with what's going on!" He let go of his weapon. The last thing he needed was an accidental discharge. He withdrew his hand from his pocket and cracked his knuckles as he waited.

"My man lost him on Montauk Highway at the Hampton Bays Diner. Some guy cut him off at the light, and when he could get through, Rick's car was nowhere in sight."

"And you couldn't send out an APB?" Jason asked, crossing his arms over his chest in an act of defiance. He was pissed as all hell.

"Think! How can I call out an APB on an investigator who's working with the department on an active B&E? How would you think that would be interpreted by my superiors?"

Jason sighed and raked a hand through his hair. "You're right. But, I'm not happy. It would have been better to have placed several of my men on his tail from the very beginning. You've made me wonder if I'm using the right men."

A shocked look crossed the officer's face. "For the record, I can tell you your sister has got all the codes and passwords necessary since the break-in. The Cloud went down, the transmissions were sent. So the money is starting to move again."

"You know I didn't want her coming in on this. But, Hailey's proved her worth to me a hell of a lot more than some other people I can think of." He glanced at Jim. Even in the dark, hidden by the tall mounds of timber being used to remodel the Bar & Grill, Jason could make out the man wasn't sure what to make of his remarks. *Good. Keep him guessing and on his toes.*

Jim blew on and took a swig of his own cup of coffee. He, too, placed it in the cup holder between them. He cleared his throat and stated, "But, *you,* my friend, have a much more serious issue to deal with."

Jason needed a jolt of caffeine and decided to take a drink. Holding the cup in his hands, he asked, "Yeah? Whatever problem that"s mine is most certainly yours, my friend."

"Not this time. You know a guy named Carl Jackson?"

Jason dropped the cup of coffee all over his pants and onto the floor. "What the—? Get me something to wipe this up with, asshole. It's hot!"

Immediately, Jim handed him a pile of Hampton Coffee napkins to blot the stain on his pants. He left the liquid and cup on the floor for Jim to pick up later.

For God's sake! How the hell did this yahoo of a cop come up with the name of a man from his inner circle? Carl normally remained under the radar. How had his name surfaced out here in the Hamptons?

Jason spoke in a level tone of voice. "Carl Jackson? No. Don't believe I know that name." From the look on Jim's face, Jason knew the man had doubts about whether or not he was telling the truth.

"HBPD had an undercover sting. One of my men saw a cop called McVey meet up with Rick at Jetty 4. When the operation was underway, McVery hacked into the squad's facial recognition software. Sure enough, the final entry was Carl Jackson, along with his rap sheet which listed *you* as his employer. But more importantly, I didn't know he trailed along with one of my men and followed Hallock into New York to meet Rick. Rick must have pegged them at the St. Regis and somehow got a photo on his phone. Hence, the ID. They're closing in on you, Rockwell. Hailey's got to drain the accounts fast and get the hell out of Dodge."

Jason was fuming. What had possessed Carl to come out of hiding? Tires crunched on the gravel outside, and headlights lit up the back windshield. "That's my ride. You stay the hell away from doing anything about Jackson. I'll take care of him. I have to figure out how we're going to get word to Hailey. You said, lately, she's surrounded by guards at the office and her apartment."

"I'll take her to dinner over at the 1770 House. This time of year, it's pretty empty. Do I have your permission? No one will question her being with the Chief of Police for a night out. Short and sweet. I'll pass the information to her and see when she thinks we can safely pull out."

Jason stewed, but at the moment he had no choice and a bigger problem on his hands. The lights on the car that pulled up flashed.

"Go ahead. But, so help, me, Jim, if you so much as lay a finger on her, I swear, I'll cut each of them off, one by one."

Jim chuckled, but Jason could tell it wasn't genuine. "I'll aim for Friday night. Go. Get out of here. The bridge is going to go up. The last thing we need to do is have to explain why we got trapped in here when the water rose."

Jason lived a shady lifestyle, always trying to be one step ahead of the law. But, if Jim Benjamin so much as touched one hair on Hailey's head, he'd send his best man calling and no one in Southampton would be the wiser.

CHAPTER NINETEEN

*T*hirsty, Thomas made his way through an extremely large crowd of people, stopping along the way to make small talk with members of the Hampton elite. These people were the farm's bread and butter, and networking, as much as he despised it, was a necessary part of the job.

Turning away from wishing Bob and Julie Windemere a belated happy anniversary, the crowd, as if on cue, parted. And there, leaning up against the bar, stood Courtney Stockton. He sucked in his breath as he beheld her in a red off-the-shoulder sequined ballgown with a slit that went from her ankles to her upper thigh. He grew hard at the mere sight of her. She moved just slightly and her red stiletto-heeled shoes caught his eye, making him move faster to be by her side. Finally next to her, his heart flip-flopped like a teenager's on a first date with the girl of his dreams.

It was then he saw the drink in her hand.

"What do you think you're doing with that?" he asked with a brotherly tone in his voice, but he certainly didn't feel that way. As he reached for Courtney's favorite drink, a Cosmopolitan, a scowl replaced the smile on his face. The drink sloshed over the glass rim and spilled onto his Gucci suit.

"Oh, how clumsy of me!" Courtney took a napkin from the bar and attempted to brush away the stain. His heart raced faster at every dab. Then he realized her hand no longer brushed away the liquid but *had come to rest on his chest. From her cheeky grin, she'd done so...on purpose.*

Placing his hand over hers, he returned her grin with one of his own. "You're always taking care of someone, aren't you?"

She stepped back and threw the napkin away. He watched in fascination as she downed the remains of her drink. She then snapped her fingers and called to the nearest bartender. "Scotch. Neat, please."

His eyebrows arched in surprise.

"What?" She moved a tad closer to him and lowered her voice. In a husky tone, she practically purred, "Don't you think I know your likes and your dislikes by now?"

Thomas tried his best to turn sideways in an attempt to hide the bulge growing in his pants at her blatant hidden sexual innuendo. He had a feeling she knew exactly what he wanted.

The bartender returned with two drinks, one for each of them.

"What shall we toast to, Tom? It's a special occasion."

She caught him off-guard. "Ah...Squirt... I don't know —"

The woman cut him off. She twirled around, trying not to spill the contents of her drink. "You can see I don't have pigtails anymore. And, I go by Courtney now, since I'm all grown up. In case you haven't noticed."

Oh, he noticed all right. What hot-blooded man wouldn't? She batted her large brown eyelashes at him. Putting her hand on her hip, she cocked her head to the side as if she was about to model for the cover of Vogue. God, she was stunning! He couldn't help but let his eyes roam the length of her body, and the imp relished in the control she had over him.

"What about to renewing old friendships?" Courtney asked. "The night's young, and this place is so....so...magical."

Her sparkling dark eyes drew him in. Looking her over once more, he stopped at the cleavage of the sweetheart neckline of her gown. He took a hearty swig of his Scotch, thinking of what lay hidden by the sexy beaded top of the dress. "What do you have in mind?"

As a member of the wait staff passed by, Courtney drained her drink, placing it on the tray the woman carried. He did the same.

Giving him a beguiling smile, she said, "The night's made for dancing. I never got a birthday present since I was studying for finals. What do you say about one dance for my gift?"

It was the perfect excuse to intertwine his left hand with hers. "You've got some kind of agenda tonight. I can see it in your eyes. Come on, Cinderella, your dance awaits. I think you may be in need of a chaperone, and I conveniently didn't bring a date." Miracles do happen. How could he have predicted he'd bump into her like this?

Drawing her out onto the floor where many couples were cheek-to-cheek, he took her in his arms and drew her to him. He leaned down and whispered in her ear, "I only dance the slow ones, if you catch my drift." He could have sworn he felt her shiver in his arms. As they moved to the tune of the slow ballad played by the orchestra, she rested her head on his chest. She smelled like lavender. The image of both of them sitting in a foaming bath flashed through his mind. She'd no idea the control she had over him. Or maybe she did, since she brushed her hips up against him.

When the music stopped, Courtney tried to move away, but he pulled her into his arms, holding her tightly by the waist. Thomas looked down into eyes filled with smoking desire. How could this be? He felt like a moth drawn to a flame "Courtney, you are..." He sounded like a blubbering fool. "You are the most beautiful woman in the room. You took my breath away the moment I saw you. I couldn't believe it was you. If you want to get out of here, I know a place where we can go that's a bit more private."

Courtney took his hand and pressed it to her cheek. She kissed his palm. "Oh, Tom — "

Beep….Beep….Beep….

What the hell? He awoke with a start. Sunlight poked through the slats of the plantation shutters of his bedroom windows. Hitting the alarm to snooze mode, he lay back, hoping to drift back to where the dream left off. Thomas's dream-induced erection ached from wanting her so badly. A cold shower was definitely in order.

Reaching for his phone, he deleted the alarm and bounded out of bed. Once he had a shower, he'd find her. He wanted answers. Grabbing the towel from the hook behind the bathroom door, he turned the knob on cold. Courtney had no idea what he had in store for her, and she *was* going to listen to him, whether she wanted to or not!

* * *

What was all that noise in his backyard? Once out of the shower, Thomas donned a pair of jeans and zipped them up. As he towel dried his hair, he opened the plantation shutters. His jaw literally hit the floor. The entire area looked like something out of the latest action movie.

From his vantage point, he eyed two snipers on top of his pool house. At least seven K-9 dogs were sniffing about the property, from the dunes to the back patio and pool. A large contingent of police and FBI agents, all dressed in flak jackets and carrying rifles, gathered poolside around a man he knew all too well.

Sam Tanner. What's he doing in Southampton? If I didn't see this with my own eyes, I'd never believe it.

His aunt's second-in-command was adamantly pointing to parts of the yard and the roof above where Tom stood. He seemed to be giving instructions to the multitude of law enforcement, and they nodded in return. The group dispersed.

Sam turned away from the house, stared up to the sky, and headed out to the beach. Thomas's jaw dropped again when Natasha, his "housekeeper," ran after him, only to enter into what seemed to be one serious conversation.

Thomas dressed as fast as humanly possible. He donned a

turtleneck, heavy knit sweater, and thrust his feet into his deck shoes.

Damn! Am I good or what? FBI, my ass. Did I not peg Courtney for CIA? And I'd bet those snipers are Special Ops from DC, courtesy of my aunt. But what the hell happened overnight?

Utmost on his mind was locating Courtney. He took it all in, turned away from the view and walked to the door. Upon opening it, he was met by two large, muscular men dressed in dark black suits. It was obvious both were packing weapons by the bulge in their coats.

Thomas took a step back. "Whoa! Who the hell are you?"

"For now," the taller man said forcefully, "we've replaced Ms. Stockton as your bodyguards."

"Why would I need to be guarded inside my own home?" No reply. "I want to talk to Sam Tanner. Get out of my way." The two men stood still, blocking the doorway. "Listen, I know Agent Tanner must be calling the shots. If you don't escort me down to him, I'm putting in a call to the Director."

The wall the men had made parted like the Red Sea.

The men identified themselves as they walked down the hall to the stairs that led to the kitchen and outdoors. "Agents Smith and Morgan, sir. Don't touch anything. Agent Tanner will explain when we get outside, but you're not going any farther than the back patio." The man spoke into his earpiece. "Night Fox on the move."

As he walked through his home, Thomas could not believe the number of people working inside. Additional security cameras were being installed. Men and women were placed strategically as guards at doorways and windows. The front door and foyer had been completely blocked off, and the kitchen served as command central.

How was it I didn't hear them coming and going during last night? On his way to bed, he'd helped himself to a cup of coffee from the pot on the stove. Thinking back, it possessed a bitter taste. Did Natasha drug him so he'd remain out of it?

"Night Fox on the patio."

Thomas followed the two men out onto the terrace and went to move to its edge to drink in more of the action around him. A firm grip on his bicep tugged him back underneath the eave.

"I want to see what's happening. I *own* this estate, in case you've forgotten." His plea got him nowhere. "Where's Agent Tanner?" As he spoke to his new bodyguards, he looked up and spied four rifles poking out from the top of the roof of his house pointing toward the beach.

Before either agent could reply, the sound of a helicopter was heard approaching the estate. Both men drew their guns and pushed Thomas behind him. He peered between the two shoulders in front of him. A black Apache chopper entered the air space on the other side of the dunes by his boardwalk. He gulped. This was indeed serious. When the chopper landed, the men did not stand down, but eased up on the grips of their weapons.

In tandem with the landing, a surfer in a hooded black wetsuit came over the dunes to stand next to Sam and Natasha on the boardwalk. Their heads huddled together, deep in conversation. The outline of the body in the wetsuit brought back memories of his licking the contours of its intimate places many years ago.

So what have we here? Courtney, Sam and Natasha. I've been played, but I have to hear her out. Find out why my house has been turned into an armed fortress overnight.

Thomas's eyes drifted from the trio to the helicopter on the beach. An older woman surrounded by six agents in blue suits came walking up the boardwalk. Aunt Elizabeth! She immediately directed Courtney's entourage to walk with her, everyone paying close attention to whatever she said. As she neared the patio, his pulse rate eased. He pushed past his guards.

"I'll deal with you later. You couldn't tell me about all this?" He directed his comments to Courtney. She stared back. He realized she had a gun strapped to the belt of her wetsuit and a rifle slung over her shoulder.

"Thomas!" Elizabeth Hallock suddenly stood in front of him. "Back off. She's doing her job. You'll know all in due time."

"I'm sorry, Auntie." He hugged her. "You can only imagine what's been running through my mind since I woke up this morning."

"You've a right to be upset. Come. Let's get out of this brisk air."

While his two guards remained at the French doors, everyone else entered the kitchen.

"Natasha, there is Earl Grey in this house, isn't there?" Even with all going on around her, his aunt grinned.

"Yes, Director. Right away. Why doesn't everyone sit down?" Natasha's eyes evaded Thomas as she walked passed him to do the Director's bidding.

Thomas called out to his "housekeeper". "I'll deal with you later, Natasha." He turned and looked at those gathered around the kitchen table. "How the hell could I not have seen this coming?" Thomas put his head in hands. Then, he realized something didn't jive. "Aunt Elizabeth, why are you here? Rick told me Joe was supposed to aid you as the middle man should he need resources from the CIA."

"Things are more serious than we thought. But, we'll settle the details later." A broad grin broke out on her face and she rummaged in her laptop bag. " I'm here because I got this invitation." She whipped out a square white paper from her bag and placed her trademark reading glasses on the tip of her nose and read, "You are cordially invited to attend the engagement party of Thomas Hallock and Courtney Stock —"

"*What?*" Courtney and Thomas both chimed out in unison.

The woman clapped her hands and smiled with glee. "Oh, I do so love a good family party! I wouldn't have missed this for the world!"

CHAPTER TWENTY

When Thomas, accompanied by Courtney, left his "engagement" party at the Hampton Beach Country Club, it was as if he'd been whisked off in a presidential motorcade. The only things missing were the flags attached to the hood of the car and decals on the doors.

Give his mother credit. The matriarch of the family went all out for the night. And no wonder; the woman had what she'd dreamed for the last twenty years – her eldest son finally finding his soul mate. How many times during the course of the evening had she told him how "thrilled" she and his father were Courtney had come back into his life? *And* the fourth of July was a perfect date to tie the knot.

The Fourth of July! Mother would try to outdo those within her Hampton social circle for the event of the season. He felt down right awful at the deception and the disappointment he'd put her through when everything ended. Mother had been in his corner ever time he'd had to deal with his father over business matters. A lioness protecting her cubs....But, maybe not, if the stars are aligned.

Even though his Aunt Elizabeth knew of the "fake" engagement, he couldn't help but feel guilty seeing the glow on her face as well. His beloved aunt beamed throughout the entire evening. Since she was known for her matchmaking skills, he'd become a bit uneasy when he caught her staring at him and his "fiancée," her eyes twinkling in delight.

Leaning back in the leather seat, he let out a sigh of relief. The intensity of the sound reverberated through the car.

"You sound as if you're really glad the party's over. The deed is done." Expecting a professional tone in Courtney's voice, he didn't hear one. Hell, hadn't this charade been her idea? Her somewhat melancholy comment made him turn to look at her. Unable to take his eyes off her all night long, he drank in her beauty one more time.

With the aid of the flashing streetlights, he saw Courtney staring into her lap. She fingered the diamond he'd placed on her left ring finger in a true romantic, knee-bending proposal in front a crowd of two hundred people.

Courtney chuckled. "Tom, you really went overboard. I can't believe the size of this cubic zirconia ring. How many supposed carats does it have?"

Thomas watched for her reaction. "It's four carats, Court. I tried to find one similar to the one you described to me that night in the cottage. You know, a large square cut surrounded by smaller diamonds."

She stiffened at his mention of that night. "Well, I've got to admit it's four carats of the best fake bling I've ever seen. I'm surprised you didn't pull out one of those huge lollipop suckers for show and effect."

"*Fake?* You think I'd put a fake ring on your hand?" Courtney's head snapped up and she turned to face him. Awe best described the look on her face. "My mother and sister would have known immediately something wasn't kosher. Those two can spot costume jewelry a mile away."

"You can't be serious." She looked as if she was about to

swoon and grabbed at her neck with her right hand.

"Damn straight. Had to call Joe and get him to get Neil Lane. He jetted into Gabreski yesterday. Rick took me to meet his plane." Thomas reached for both of her hands and brought them to his lips.

"Really?" Courtney tried to pull her hands from his, but he held firm to both. Her voice squeaked. "But he's the man who chooses the ring for the man on the TV dating show."

Thomas nodded. "He's outfitted the next generation of Hallocks very nicely. Kate and Megan were over the moon with theirs. I couldn't break with tradition."

Courtney moved to the edge of the seat, her hands still in his. She squeezed his fingers hard. "Thomas, *this*," she nodded at the ring, "isn't for real. Don't make this anything more than it is. I'm going back underground as soon as we capture the people who took your money and planted a bomb somewhere near one of your properties. You've got to take that threat very seriously. I thought you fully understood the basic schematics at the briefing after your aunt landed and we filled you in."

No more role-playing the part of a loving and doting fiancée for her. Now, she was back. Agent Courtney Stockton. Not for much longer, if he had anything to say about it.

Raul opened the privacy window. "We're home."

Looking through the windows, Thomas saw both sets of lead and follow cars had pulled up in front of the estate. As an armed officer approached the vehicle, Courtney shook off his hold. She reached to the floor, drew her gun and set it on her lap, her finger on its trigger.

"What the hell are you doing?" he whispered.

"You can't be too careful. Rick thinks there's a mole. It could be anyone. Even here."

The bile rose in Thomas's throat at the mere thought. He'd sat at the dining room table that afternoon listening to his aunt toss out names and places. Knowing now that Hailey lied in her interview and there seemed to be a link to Jason Rockwell, his blood boiled. His head still spun with all he'd been told of what transpired. Thank heavens some of the details, such as the bomb, were not brought up within the confines of the Hallock family mansion. His mother had commented on the added security when they'd danced, but he assured her it was necessary with the Board being in town and the monies still not recovered.

"Thomas!" Courtney shook his shoulder. He roused himself from his musings. "Get out of the car and stay surrounded by the guards. I'm right behind you."

He did as he was told, his heart racing in his chest. Knowing Courtney was nearby, he reached out for the courage to make it to the front door. Within seconds, a soft hand covered his own.

Thomas turned and arched his eyebrows in surprise, quickly pulling his hand away. "What the -?"

Natasha, dressed in combat gear, drew up next to him. "No Russian, boss. Court's got to go over the night ops with Raul. She'll be inside in a minute." The woman rubbed his back. "Hey, if Court's got your back, you're going to be okay. Trust me. She saved me more than once."

The front door opened, and Thomas entered his house, followed by the four guards that walked him inside. Courtney had given him something to think about. Who could he trust?

"I'm thinking you could use a Scotch." Natasha headed toward the den. "And that woman's going to need a drink to calm her nerves. Got to find the Baileys. You know, it's not every night a woman gets engaged to the man of her dreams."

With that comment, his "housekeeper" was out of sight. Had he heard Natasha correctly? "The man of her dreams?" Well, then. It might be one-thirty in the morning, but the night was still young in his book. Thomas had plans.

* * *

Cupsogue Beach
Dune Road

Shifting the Jeep into four-wheel drive, Rick maneuvered the SUV into the campgrounds of the county park. Driving from the asphalt parking lot onto the sandy beach road was tricky, the back of the vehicle swaying as the tires gripped the sand as he down-shifted. In the rush to get to his meeting, he hadn't thought to let the air out from the tires to make the drive easier. Even with his windows rolled up, he heard the winds howl. Waves crested over the small dunes.

He pulled in behind a long RV parked next to a familiar black Ford truck with a roof rack. Getting out, he pulled his anorak up around his ears and looked about. The place was deserted. Rick didn't spook easily, but somehow the atmosphere lent itself to Halloween. He'd come for an answer to a message he'd sent that afternoon. The return call to meet Danny McVey came at midnight. With hundreds of guests viewing Thomas's "proposal" to his sister, Rick had the perfect diversion to slip away from the crowds. Making his way out through the kitchen, he went unnoticed by the club's workers busy preparing to serve the cake and champagne.

Rick rapped his knuckle in code on the door. Hearing light footsteps approach, he reached for his gun as a precautionary measure. If Danny wasn't the one opening the door, he'd be ready.

The blustery burst of wind rushed in, catching them both off-guard. Both men lost control of their grip on the door, and it slammed into the side of the camper. Rick immediately grabbed for the door, entered the camper and closed it behind him. Danny stepped away from the entrance and lowered his body to sit on the floor in the small kitchen area. With what had gone down in the drug sting, it made sense Danny had to stay incognito. But, to act like this? The fact that the cop was sitting on the floor with his gun in his lap sent a chill down Rick's spine…and there was *no one*, not a soul, within a half a mile of the entrance to the park. What the hell?

"You came alone? Sure no one followed you?" Danny asked in rapid succession as he sat in the darkness.

A flash of moonlight filtered in through the blinds as the wind buffered the trailer, allowing Rick to see the layout of the trailer. He double-latched the door and sat opposite the man who'd taken on two very big risks on his behalf. "If you're acting like this, I've got a feeling I'm not going to like what you found out."

"I think my cover is blown."

"What?" Rick stared at the man, dumbfounded. "Why do you think that?"

"When I went out on that sting? I came back late that night to the HBPD office. I found my computer moved on my desk. Its laptop's history showed someone hacked in. Whoever did it saw I'd used the facial recognition database. I was sure I'd closed everything out and hadn't left a cyber trail."

"So, someone knows and is probably asking a lot of questions about why you want to know about Carl Jackson." Once more, the dread of what Rick feared for Thomas crawled up his spine. He shivered, not just from the cold, damp air in the RV. What Danny told him was the final nail in the coffin. "You're about to tell me Rockwell and Jim are in this together."

Danny set his gun to the side and ran his fingers through his hair. "When you sent me that encrypted message, your friend, Joe, let me access some files. I was able to find the link that put the two together. Those two have been shadow friends since high school days. No one here ever knew Jim worked for NYPD as a rookie. That's when he hooked up with Jason again and met Jackson. Jim got tossed off the force for 'conduct unbecoming.' I dug deeper, found someone who was in Jim's squad at the time, seemed to recall it had to do with half a dozen women screaming about sexual harassment: some coworkers, some perps he felt up while 'looking for contraband.' His lawyer got One-PP to seal his file so he could move on. A slap on the wrist, if you ask me. So lucky us, the man made his way out here and worked his way up the ranks. My take is, he and Rockwell are out to finish Tom off. Bankrupt him. Jim just seems to be after the money, Rick. But, for Rockwell, it's more personal. And both of them will do anything, hurt anyone, who gets in their way. That puts your sister as a prime target right now, thanks to her new fiancé."

Rick pounded his head back against the kitchen's tiny cabinet. "I've got to get out of here and get them sequestered for good." He went to stand, but Danny pulled him to his knees. Rick had one more question to ask. "Were you able to get any intelligence regarding the bomb?"

"No, but I do know Jim is not happy he's being overridden on requests for SWAT teams, bomb sniffing dogs and robots. Rumor has it he nearly had apoplexy in the office yesterday." Suddenly, Danny's body went rigid. Placing his hand to his lips, he rose slowly and made his way to the bedroom window, motioning for Rick to remain in place.

Rick listened, but all he heard was the wind and the pounding of the surf. Danny's reaction had the hairs standing on the back of his neck.

"How'd you get here?" Rick whispered.

Danny returned and squatted down beside him. "I came in by kayak. It was a rough crossing, but nothing I can't handle. Listen, you've got a gun?"

Rick nodded, tapping his pocket.

"Good. Keep it on you. Go home. Be sure Courtney and Thomas stay put. Have your guys found any trace of the monies?"

"Anthony said it was discovered this afternoon there's a pattern to deposits and withdrawals to both Rockwell's and Jim's accounts. Troy was lucky enough to stumble onto a code name using number palindromes and anagrams of letters."

Danny placed his hand on his arm. "There's only one thing for me to do. I can't help anymore. I can't take the chance. I told the PD shrink I'm burned out and taking vacation time. People close to me think I'm heading to California, but I'm heading out of the country. The Director has a job for me, and I've taken her up on it."

Momentarily stunned, Rick realized Danny had outlived his usefulness and placed himself in jeopardy. If anything happened to the young cop, Rick would never forgive himself.

Rick rose and stood against the door. "I can't thank you enough. Can't I give you a ride into town?"

Danny shook his head. "No. Got to do this my way."

Rick understood. Protocol. Bracing for the onslaught of the wind, he held tight to the door when he opened it, and closed it tightly in place when he left. He hopped into his Jeep and left the county park, making his way slowly along Dune Road, being sure to do the thirty-mile-per-hour speed limit.

Just as he was about a half a mile from the Sunfish Beach Club, he caught a police light flashing in his rearview mirror. He looked around for other emergency vehicles and pulled over to the side of the two-land road. Perhaps the cop had received a call and was making his way into town. But as he parked on the side of the road, so did the patrol car. The tinted windows of the Jeep made it hard to ascertain the identity of the cop who had come up on the driver's side of the car, motioning him to roll down his window. Puzzled, he did as requested.

A bright light from the officer's flashlight blocked his field of vision. The voice that spoke, along with the cold butt of a pistol placed alongside his temple, sent shock waves through his system.

"You've gone one step too far, Rick. Get out of the car."

"Jim, you've got this wrong. What the hell are you doing? For Christ's sake, I was doing the speed limit." *Play stupid, dumb. Anything. Think! You've got to get the upper hand!*

The gun pressed deeper into his skull.

"I-told-you-to-get-out-of-the-car. Or your brains are going to be splattered all over the windshield."

Rick had no choice. Once he stepped onto the road, Jim tossed him onto the hood of the police car and frisked him. The Glock Rick had stuffed into the pocket of his rain jacket was taken from him.

"Packing, are you? Just who did you meet down at Cupsogue? I hear Danny McVey and you have been keeping company."

Rick wouldn't give Jim the satisfaction of a reply.

"Don't want to talk? Well, I've got a few people who want some answers from you. They have a nasty way of getting them if you don't cooperate."

After shackling Rick in handcuffs, Jim opened the back door of the police car. Grabbed by the sleeve of his coat, Rick toppled onto the back seat, bumping into a large, burly mass of a figure whose face lit up at the sight of him.

"Imagine meeting you in a place like this, Stockton. God, I have to hand it to my sister. When she says you sniff at clues like a hound dog looking for a good bone hiding in the dirt, she ain't kidding."

Sucking in his breath, Rick felt the sweat break out on his brow. Jason Rockwell!

Jason called out to Jim. "Move it. I've got people that want to meet Rick tonight. Lights flashing. You know where to go. I've got the master key, thanks to my sister."

Rick had all he could do to keep from swiveling his head to look at his companion in the back seat. *The master key!*

Pedal to the metal, the cruiser shot out from the curb, lights flashing. Cuffed with his hands behind his back, Rick leaned against the headrest. His mind whirled with "What-if" scenarios. He prayed the Jeep would be discovered soon by the HBPD patrol that made the beach road night round at one. And that Danny McVey would check in with the Director before heading out of Hampton Beach. If he was lucky, both would possibly coincide at the same time.

At the moment, however, he was in the midst of the perfect storm. Rick was being swallowed up by the highest wave of corruption he'd ever dealt with in his entire career.

CHAPTER TWENTY-ONE

Surprised to find Tom's study empty and dark, Courtney headed for the family room. She'd hoped to find him sitting behind his desk enjoying a Scotch. God knew he had earned one. It was crucial they talk, and not about the "grand gesture." There was plenty of time for *that* discussion later.

As she turned the corner in the hallway, she bumped into Natasha.

"Tash! Where did Tom go? I thought you were going to give him a drink and he'd be in the study."

Natasha juggled two Baileys on the rocks in her hands. "I don't know where he disappeared to. I did as you asked. He downed the first in one swallow, then asked for another. The last I saw he was heading in the direction of the media room. Said he wanted to see you when you finally came inside. Here." She thrust the tumbler at Courtney. "You look like you—"

Courtney bobbled the drink in her right hand while the woman grabbed for the other. "Girlfriend, is that what I think it is? A *real* four-carat Neil Lane diamond!" Tash squealed. She held Courtney's hand up almost to her nose to ogle the ring. Draining her own drink, she whistled then said, "You sure do know how to pick them."

Courtney dislodged her hand from Natasha's. "Ah, before you think you're going to be my maid of honor, let me just state for the record the man went overboard as far as I am concerned. However, he did tell me his mother and sister could spot a fake a mile away. For the record, that made sense. Very convincing."

"But *four* carats?" Natasha stood stunned. "Did he do the whole 'down on one knee' thing too?"

Taking Natasha by the elbow, Courtney directed her friend to the kitchen.

"Yup. He did. It was so romantic, just like I'd always dreamed of." A loud sigh escaped her lips.

Natasha's eyebrows rose in surprise.

Oh, what did I just do? Tash can read me like a book! She's one of the few that knows what happened. But, I never told her Tom's the only man who mattered in my life. How many times did she try to set me up and not understand why things never worked?

Courtney sipped her drink and leaned against the counter, her eyes downcast. She couldn't meet her former partner face-to-face. Emotionally, it had been a rough night. Her dreams played out in front of her for "real" at the country club, her heart beat with the love she'd tried so unsuccessfully to eradicate through the years. But now back in reality, she was Cinderella, dressed in rags at the fireplace, brushing up the ash.

"Court!"

She lifted her head to see concern etched on Natasha's face. She drained her drink and held out the tumbler. "One more for the road. I have to find Tom and talk."

"You okay? You look as if you've lost your favorite puppy. Is it Tom?"

"Just fill the drink up, damn it!" Courtney didn't mean to sound curt.

Natasha came over to her, bottle in hand, and filled the glass.

"Whoa. I hit a nerve. Something's going on. I have a feeling I can put my finger on it, but you look like you don't need to go into it right now."

Courtney merely nodded and stated, "Later. I promise." She drained her second glass of Baileys and set it on the counter. "Where do you think he is?"

"I'll find out." Natasha spoke into her earpiece. "He told the guard in the media room he was heading off to bed. To tell you he'd see you in the morning. Court, just my opinion, but, go easy on him. Tom seemed angry, but beaten up."

"Copy that, girlfriend."

Hugging her best friend, she decided she, too, needed some shuteye. Even though dawn would come early, four hours of sleep was better than none. She walked out of the kitchen and climbed the stairs to her bedroom. Stopping at every other stair, she glanced down to stare at the ring on her finger and remembered the words he'd said as he placed it on her finger.

If only the man hadn't turned his back on her so many years ago. If only she'd never run. If only she'd never joined the CIA. If only…

* * *

Knowing sunrise would soon be upon her, Courtney finished brushing her teeth. She was too weary and tired to take the time to wipe off her makeup and undo her hair. Taking one last look at her red sequined ball gown, she unzipped the back and let it fall to the floor. Her bra, lacy panties and stockings followed close behind, Taking her robe from the back of the bathroom door, she switched off the light and walked into the darkness of her bedroom. Why turn on the light if she was only going to climb under the comforter? She was so bone tired, she'd be asleep within minutes.

She stopped in her tracks. Her phone! Forget it. It was in her evening purse in the bathroom, and she didn't have the energy to go back and retrieve it. Besides, the minute the sun broke the horizon, she'd be awake. Her body had its own clock, especially since she was back on a job.

Letting out a loud yawn, she pulled back the bedding and slid onto the crisp sheets. Nestling into the middle of the king size bed, she sighed, pulling the blankets over her head, and rolled onto her right side.

"Do I say good night or good morning, beautiful?" Tom's husky voice echoed in the room. His arm snaked out and pulled her up against him, and the memory of his unclothed body flashed through her mind.

His warm hand on her naked waist sucked the air out of her. The feel of her nipples brushing up against his chest shot a tingling sensation to every part of her body. She couldn't speak. His hand moved, his fingers brushing up and down her side, before coming to a halt under her breast. His forefinger circled her nipple, pinching it lightly. A shiver rocketed through her, causing her body to betray her. She moved closer, wanting to touch him, her skin to his.

Realizing what she was about to do, she jerked away, only to be held more firmly in place. Why was she not pushing at him, telling him he had to go, leave? This couldn't happen. Not now. Not ever again.

Courtney did *not* trust herself. Her emotions had been on an emotional roller coaster, culminating in the ride of her life tonight.

"Tom, no! What —?" Courtney's plea was silenced by his lips covering hers. He nibbled lightly on her lower lip. She struggled to argue her point, but when she opened her mouth, his tongue entered…and she remembered. *Everything.* How he touched. How he'd made her feel. How he made love. With one stroke, one caress, the wetness was there between her thighs. Only he made her feel this intense, on the border of an orgasm without going any farther.

Trying to clear her brain from its love-induced fog, her thoughts warred against each other.

No! You can't do this. Yes, go for it! For once, think of yourself. Take the night. Treasure what he wants to give you tonight. There will never be another time for the two of you ever again.

Surrendering to her feelings, setting her objectivity aside, she brought her hand up to lovingly caress the side of his face. Oh, how she'd missed him.

"Thomas," she whispered, a smile broke out on her face. Her battle to keep him at bay was over. She wanted him, if only for the night.

"Courtney," he reached for her hand and kissed and suckled each finger. Tom threw his leg over hers, and as his penis brushed up against her belly, hard and ready, he groaned. "I want to be inside you. When you ran from me, I searched forever to find you. I —"

She'd heard enough. Bringing her arms up and around his neck, she drew him to her, their bodies melding in a perfect fit. She kissed him with all the passion she possessed, and he returned each kiss with one deeper than the last. Suddenly, she found herself flipped onto her back, her hands entwined with Tom's, straddling both sides of her head on the pillow. He towered over her, his dark eyes smoldering with desire.

"You are as stunning and breathtaking as I remember. When you came down those stairs tonight in that red sequined gown..." His voice trailed off as his mouth went to work, first planting a kiss on her lips. He proceeded to make a trail of kisses from her mouth, down the side of her neck, ending by circling her nipple. When he bit and suckled it playfully, Courtney moaned, her hips jerking off the bed. She wanted him in her. She didn't want to come unless they shared the union.

Spreading her legs, she offered him the invitation he desperately wanted. Desire was written all over his face, along with the fact he, like she, couldn't hold out much longer.

"Please," Courtney pleaded. "I need you now. I love you."

With one swift push, Tom filled her. She gasped, remembering, knowing it would only get better. Breaking the clasp he had had on her hands, she wrapped them around his waist and pulled him into her, deeper. She spread her legs wider. "Faster, Cowboy. There's a few more hours for us to do this slower and get it right."

"We always got it right that night, Court. Each time, better than the last." He panted in her ear.

Within seconds, a burst of pleasure exploded from her vagina and wrapped around her heart as Tom spilled his seed. She let go and rolled to her side, wrapping her legs around him to hold him in place as the pulsing subsided. She felt whole, replenished, satisfied.

Even in the dark, she could read a questioning look on his face. "What is it? Did I do something wrong?"

"Oh, God, no. You were…perfect. Sound a bit cliché?" As she shook her head no, he tapped the tip of her nose. "Did I hear you right? Did you, Courtney Ellen Stockton, tell me you loved me?"

In the heat of the moment, she'd slipped. She'd never hear the end of it, knowing the man in her bed. Shivering from the coolness in the air, she drew the comforter up and over the two of them. Her choice of words was critical. She loved this man. And from all the moments they shared since she returned, there was no doubt that should she have stayed in Hampton Beach, things would have turned out differently. But one can't look back. Only forward. Tom had to be told, in the gentlest of terms, there could be no "happily ever after." She was due back in Positano. And the mere thought of doing so broke her heart.

Snuggling into his warm body, she said, "Tom, you and I have so much to – "

Bang! Bang! Bang!

"What the fuck?" Tom sat up, drawing the comforter up and over the two of them. "Who the hell's pounding on your door at this hour?"

"Come in!" Courtney shouted.

The door flung open and Natasha rushed in. She came to a dead halt. Her eyes lit on Tom then to Courtney then back to Tom again. "Well, I'm glad you're both getting some sleep."

Courtney knew deep in her bones something serious had transpired.

"What is it? What's happened? Spit it out."

"Partner, I've been trying to reach you by phone for the last fifteen minutes. I got a call from Reggie. Rick was due for a briefing with Sarah and his team at 2. He didn't show. His car was found abandoned on Dune Road. CSU found Jim Benjamin's fingerprints on his car window."

The minute Natasha said Rick hadn't shown for the briefing, Courtney flew out of bed, giving no thought to Tom. She threw on her clothes and dug her Sig Sauer out of the dresser drawer. Checking to be sure it was fully loaded, she slid the weapon into her shoulder holster.

"Wait!" Tom went to brush aside the blanket to get out of bed. He had a determined look on his face. "I'm going with you."

"No! Don't even go there." Courtney held her hand up to ward him off. The "don't you dare cross me on this" look she sent his way had him crawling back under the sheets.

"Where's Sarah?" Courtney grabbed hold of Natasha and

headed for the door.

"Outside. She's got what you need."

Courtney turned back to where she'd just made love to the man of her dreams. "I'll be back. You can count on it."

"Court? I love you. Go get my best friend."

"Ditto, I love you,too. And for the record, I always have."

What she'd stated had the desired effect. Thomas was indeed shocked. Courtney didn't have time left to explain, as much as she wanted to. She closed the door, following Natasha down the front staircase.

Outside she found Sarah waiting as Tash had stated, the Land Rover's engine idling. The unknown loomed before her with the stakes high. Jumping in the car, she fastened her seat belt. One nod to Sarah and the vehicle took off down the drive. Jim Benjamin meant Jason Rockwell. Jason Rockwell meant that she, thank God, held the ultimate trump card and could finally put it into play. Holding on as the car weaved and swerved around the lanes at a breakneck speed, Courtney prayed silently they'd arrive in time.

CHAPTER TWENTY-TWO

Sag Harbor

"I can't believe Jason chose this active work site of all places to conduct business in the dead of night. Someone will be coming by to check. There's got to be security guards stationed on all four corners of the property." Sarah blew out a sigh of disgust.

"The men are, no doubt, on Jason's payroll, whether it be through the cops or a private firm." Looking through her night vision goggles, Courtney made out men stationed in the positions Sarah had pointed out. "The project manager's trailer is too conspicuous." She zeroed in on two vehicles parked on the dark side of the trailer. "The cars parked off to the side? One is an unmarked STPD patrol car. The other's a Lincoln. Jim and Jason are definitely here. Rick's got to be inside."

A feminine voice spoke up from the back seat of the Land Rover. "I don't think those two would be stupid enough to hide your brother there. Somebody checking to see what was going on at this time of night would wonder why the lights were on and call for backup. My guess is he's in that old warehouse the builder is tearing down to make way for the new condominiums."

Sarah's and Courtney's eyes were drawn to a shiny key that had emerged, twirling between the woman's thumb and forefinger.

Courtney eyed the object momentarily stunned by what she saw. "Hailey? Is that what I think it is?" She raised her hand up in hopes her agent in the back seat would give her a chance for a better look.

The office manager, dressed in black from head to toe, laid the key in Courtney's hand. "Yup, the master key. I made two. One for me. One for you."

Sarah whistled then said, "I'll be damned. How'd you come by that?"

"Well, it's certainly not the real one. I had a chance to make a copy this afternoon. Jason wasn't the wiser. My brother hasn't doubted my allegiance through his entire scam. It's for the door to that building behind the trailer. He asked me to check out the warehouse and make sure it was stocked for the meeting tonight with his partners."

Courtney's eyes followed Hailey's finger to the side entrance of a rundown building to the left of the project engineer's trailer. This was the first she'd heard of dealing with more than two people. Knowing no one had predicted Rick being abducted, there had been little time to plan, much less communicate. The Director demanded an immediate radio silence in case their frequencies were monitored. Had Hailey not been on their side from the very beginning, the Ops team would have known nothing.

"Partners?" Sarah asked. "How many do you think he expects? In case you haven't noticed, there's only the three of us."

Hailey brushed aside Sarah's valid concerns. "A few main men, those with the most to lose. Court, this meeting's to talk about the blocked servers and the monies no longer flowing into the offshore accounts. Jason's men want answers, and he doesn't have anything to give. I do. That's why you have to let me go in. I can pretend to try to hack over the passwords on the computer with the code words Troy gave me. It will buy you two time to get on the inside."

Hailey made perfect sense. But there was a problem. Courtney had no one to run it by. Protocol called for her to speak to Agent Tanner or the Director. That wasn't going to happen. *She* had to make the call.

One quick glance over her shoulder told her exactly how to proceed. When Hailey dove into the elements of her mission, she didn't let anything stand in her way. In a short amount of time, she had turned into a great CIA agent.

A small smile formed at the corners of her mouth. Courtney thought of the training session she'd been part of at the l'arm as Hailey convinced her brother she had to "backpack through Europe for a year with friends before joining corporate America." The company gave her an encrypted phone to set up rigged calls to check in with him, while she'd spent the last year going through the paces from rookie to certified field agent. Hailey was one of the few who'd passed sniper training on the first try. The Director had reeled in one of her finest assets in the last five years, knowing there was the perfect place to embed her. Courtney agreed. When told Hailey was in place at Tom's office, the two could pull off their end of the subterfuge. In both the Agency and FBI's eyes, Jason was a mighty big fish to reel in, but to bring down the corrupt head of the Southampton Town Police Department along with him would be a major coup.

A rustling of a change of clothes could be heard coming from the back seat.

Sarah spoke up. "Court, you're calling the shots here. Say

something. You're going to let her go in there?"

"Hailey's right, Sarah. She's got to go in as if nothing is different and try to divert Jason and whoever the hell else is in there."

"But, we haven't the faintest idea how many we're facing." There was a roughness to Sarah's tone. "Listen, I go where you go, but we need more ammo."

Hailey spoke up. Courtney looked at the woman in the back seat of the SUV. She had changed into her street clothes, her face totally devoid of camouflage cream with a hint of makeup. "Once I'm in, you're going to wait fifteen minutes, then follow. When you let yourselves in, there's a closet on the right about halfway down the hall. It's padlocked. Here's that key." She passed a smaller key to Courtney. "There are two rifles and several rounds of ammo for your weapons. Word to the wise; the door creaks. When you make it to the end of the hallway, you've got to stay low even though there are piles of old lumber. Not much to hide behind. When you hear 'Secure,' I'm telling you there's only a few people to deal with. Courtney, from there you call the shots. But, if you hear 'Damn it,' get the hell out of the warehouse. Jason won't harm me and if somebody tries, he'll have men on the inside there to take care of me."

"You really okay with this, Court?" Sarah's eyes pierced hers, her eyebrows arched as if to ask, "can we really trust this woman?"

With her stomach in a quiver, Courtney spoke in a calmer tone of voice than she felt. "Hailey's not a rogue agent, Sarah. Are you armed, Hailey?"

"No gun."

"What? You can't go in there without some form of a weapon."

"Relax. I've got two lipsticks that can deliver several doses of sedatives if I need them. And a knife that flips out from my nail file. His 'friends' will check me when I go in. I'll figure out a way to let you know if Rick is among the group that's gathered. I've gotta go. I'm late."

Hailey climbed out of the black Land Rover and made her way across Bear Street, staying in the shadows as much as possible. Four blocks down from where Courtney and Sarah parked, Hailey climbed into a small car, revved its engine, did a U-turn and came back, passing them by. As she neared the condo project, she turned out her headlights as she entered the construction zone. She parked her car alongside her brother's.

Courtney let out a deep breath as Hailey unlocked the side door and made her way into the building. Glancing at her watch, she turned to Sarah.

"Be ready on my mark to go at 0300."

* * *

Long Wharf Pier
Sag Harbor

The longer time passed, the more Thomas stewed as he sat in the back seat of Reggie's Ford pickup truck alongside Joe MacAllister. He was a man who liked action – go in, get the job done, get out. As far as he was concerned, Sam Tanner and Reggie were taking far too long to assess the situation at the warehouse.

"How'd you find out where the girls were headed, Joe?" Sam asked as he sat in the driver's seat. Reggie diligently used his telescopic binoculars to focus in on the entrance to the warehouse. So far, there'd been no signs of Courtney, Sarah or Hailey.

Hailey Rockwell! Well, hadn't that come as a sucker punch

to his midsection when, on the ride over, Sam explained he'd "employed" an undercover CIA operative within his Southampton office! In reality, Thomas shouldn't be surprised with the world his aunt operated. His very existence for being in the truck, and not back at his mansion, was the fact Sam had overridden the Director. They needed someone who could shoot. Unbeknownst to many in the family, he was trained to function in an operation. It had been *years* since he'd worked an investigation for the CIA, but he knew from the look Sam's face Thomas had violated the number one protocol rule in the manual – emotional involvement with a subject/operative in a sting. Had the man truly no think it could be a possibility when he and the Director had returned Courtney to work the mission when they both knew what had driven her away in the first place?

Joe chimed in, breaking Thomas's train of thought. "Hailey called me two days ago, Sam, when her brother gave her the master key." The man's Irish brogue grew thicker the more excited he became as he told the tale. "It all started to click. Tonight, when Rick was kidnapped, all the pieces fell together. I'd done some checking on Interpol regarding Jason's crew, especially Jackson. When I realized Rick had stumbled onto the connection as well…"

"Listen." Tom was growing impatient with not being on the move. "I know your intel is critical, but when are we going in after Courtney? Has anyone forgotten the possibility she, Sarah and Hailey are walking into a trap? One that might very well blow sky-high?" His heart raced at the very thought. Hell, he'd lain awake every night, tossing and turning at the mere thought of his family or Courtney being hurt by some lunatic.

"If you don't think you can operate with a clear head and nerves of steel, you're going to stay right where you are, Tom." Sam's voice was terse and commanding. "We're to follow them in as backup. Hailey's set up some sort of diversion until we can uncover what's going on. The girls are going in first."

Reggie suddenly sat up straight in his seat. Thomas followed the man's line of sight. Reggie trained his binoculars on the side of the building.

"Hush," Reggie admonished him. "Sam, the lassies are making for the door." A few minutes passed in dead silence as they lay in wait to see what the girls would do. Dropping his binoculars, Thomas saw the man secure his gun. "Let's roll. They're inside."

Thomas took in a deep breath and exhaled. He counted to ten.

"Lock and load," Sam ordered. "Move out. Keep your eyes peeled for anything unusual." He turned to Thomas. "And you...follow orders."

Thomas didn't need to be told twice. All the men wore flak jackets covering the traditional black Agency issued pants, jackets and caps. Once out of the truck, they crossed the street. Ducking under the opening in a twelve-foot-tall chain link fence, all four men hugged the wall of the side of the crumbling exterior to the warehouse. Arriving at the door where Courtney's team had entered only moments earlier, Sam jiggled the door knob. Locked.

"Allow me." Thomas stepped forward, drawing a small black leather case from his pocket. He set about picking the lock. In one smooth move, in the dead of night, he heard the tumbler click. The door was open.

"Glad to see ye haven't lost your touch, lad," Joe whispered.

Sam shot a look at Thomas, who stared him down. He knew the pecking order of an operation. Agent Tanner was lead agent. Thomas had news for him. If push came to shove and Courtney was in danger, he was going to save her *first*.

Thomas turned to his fellow agents. "Follow Sam. Get

inside. I've a feeling in my bones, something's not right."

CHAPTER TWENTY-THREE

Courtney hadn't anticipated how dark the hallway would be as she and Sarah made their way to the closet. Both women ran their hands along the wall until finally Sarah's fingers grabbed hold of the lock.

"Found it!" she called out.

Wishing her partner spoke in a less enthusiastic tone, she prayed the reverberation had not made its way to the large open room she spied approximately five hundred feet away. Male and feminine voices were heard chattering back and forth. Hailey's plan to create a diversion hopefully had worked. Taking the key out of her pocket, she pushed Sarah to the side. She inserted the key, and the lock gave way. She placed the padlock into her pocket and shoved the key inside her sock. No one would think to look for it there, should they be discovered. At least, she hoped not.

The closet door opened, as if by magic, leaving both women stunned at the sight of what they found on the shelf in front of them.

There were no guns or rifles. No ammo as promised. *Only the digital readout of a ticking bomb set in a silver case. Courtney had triggered the timing mechanism when she opened the lock!*

"Courtney." Sarah's voice quivered. "What do we do?"

The tension of the moment, along with the reading on the clock, had Courtney dabbing at the sweat breaking out on her brow. She had to remain calm and in control. Situations similar to this had occurred in her past, but this bomb was unlike any she'd seen before. Judging from its clock, she had less than thirty minutes to do what needed to be done.

"Sarah. I'm going to lock—"

Both women whirled, caught off-guard, as the door behind them slammed shut.

"Look who we have here, Lucas." The man cocked his gun and aimed it at Courtney's chest. "I gather these are the two stragglers Jim and Mr. Jason have been waiting for. Tap them down and strip them of their weapons."

The other man did as instructed, pulling Sarah's Glock and Courtney's Sig Sauer from their respective shoulder harnesses. He ran his hands up and down both their legs. Courtney stifled a gasp as his hand brushed the spot where the key lay hidden in the thickness of her sock.

"Move! Down the hall!" The taller of the two men shoved Courtney and Sarah into the direction of the opening.

The chatter Courtney heard earlier had ceased. As they walked into the large, dank room, the first person she laid eyes on was her brother. Rick was tied to a chair, his face bruised and bleeding.

"Rick!" The next thing Courtney knew she was on the floor, her temple aching, the result of a hit by the butt of the gun from the man next to her.

"Tie them up. I've got questions to ask. I'm working on a limited amount of time." Jim Benjamin sounded furious.

As she rose from the floor, she looked up and noted Hailey's hands cuffed in front of her. Someone found out the girl's cover and Courtney had sent her walking right into a trap!

The Chief's eyes sought out Courtney's. "So, Agent Stockton. You didn't think we'd find out you planted Jason's sister in the office. Quite a slip-up on your part, wouldn't you say? Getting rusty in your old age. Jason's men found out those were fake passwords to make the money flow again. Tom's aunt must take us for fools."

"Benjamin! Keep your mouth shut and tie them up. My partners have the answers they need." Jason Rockwell bid farewell to a group of three men who left via a side door and came back to stand next to his sister.

Courtney gasped at the sound of the palm of his hand meeting Hailey's face. The woman didn't flinch.

Jason was enraged. "You betrayed me, you bitch! I did everything I could to give you a life different than mine. I wanted you to have the world. *This* is how you pay me back?" Hailey stood mute, her eyes downcast.

While Jason and Jim focused on Hailey, Courtney tried to find a way to get Sarah's attention. It was hard to do, nestled in the dark corner.

"Psst, Sarah." The girl was blindfolded, her arms tied behind her back, her feet to the chair. Courtney was bound up in the same fashion but she'd been afforded the opportunity to see her captives. It was Rick who caught her eye, cocking his head to where she and Sarah had just entered.

Hidden behind the stacks of old lumber, she made out two figures – Joe MacAllister and Reggie Litchfield and the outline of two more a bit farther back.

Joe gave her the signal that he was ready to move in. If only he knew his crew was literally sitting on a ticking bomb. Each minute that ticked off was one less to get the case out of the building and into the harbor.

Jim had come to stand in front of her.

"What are you looking at?" There's no one around for miles

who can help you and your precious brother now. Half my force is busy guarding Tom's family and the mansion. The way the man sneered and snickered sent chills down her spine. She just had to keep his attention on her a little while longer.

"You killed Janie Walker, didn't you? She got in your way, found out your plans—"

Smack! The crack of his hand hitting her jaw sent her head spinning. It was all Joe needed. It was all Joe needed to make his move.

"STPD!"

"FBI!"

A chorus of yells went up as Joe and Reggie entered the room with a bevy of agents. "Toss your weapons on the ground. Hands in the air."

Jason put his hand in his pocket, and a shot rang out. Down he went, writhing in pain. Joe sauntered over and pulled a small caliber pistol from the scumbag's pocket.

"Get up off your sorry arse, you good-for-nothing weasel. It's nothing more than a flesh wound... Cuff 'im," Joe commanded the officer next to him and strode away. With the bulk of Jason and Jim's crew rounded up, Courtney called out to Reggie who'd come to their aid.

"Reggie. The bomb! It's here!"

All heads, including those of the two she'd seen silhouetted behind Joe and Reggie, swiveled to look at her. Her jaw sagged when her eyes fell upon the last person she expected to see. *Thomas!* What the hell was he doing here? Oh, heads were going to roll if she made it back in one piece! Somebody hadn't done his job, keeping the Director's nephew in lockdown at the mansion.

Rubbing her wrist from chafing at the Flex-cuffs she'd been forced to wear, she stood as Reggie cut her loose. Taking off at a sprint, she passed Thomas, who reached out to stop her, but she evaded his grasp.

Over her shoulder she yelled out, "I love you! For once in your life, do as you're told!"

Sprinting down the hallway, Joe followed close behind.

"How much time?" Joe panted as she stopped abruptly.

"Eight minutes." Opening the closet door, her eyes fell on the display. "No time for SWAT, even if they were on the grounds. We couldn't get everyone out. What do we do?"

"Make for the water. Get it out of the building. If it blows... well, it's part of the risk and you know it."

Courtney nodded, knowing full well what she'd taken on. With her heart pounding in her ears, she sealed the deal by closing the case and clicking the clasps in place. Now for the final count. Five blocks to the pier, a normal ten minute jog. Courtney tucked it under one arm.

"Stay here."

Joe didn't argue with her, but he opened the door of the warehouse and watched her run. And run she did. Making it to the edge of the wharf, she heaved the case up into the air, but not far enough to make it out over the water. She turned to run as the bomb and watched in horror as the bomb began its descent – right toward the grand Caribou yacht...and her.

∗ ∗ ∗

The building shook so hard the glass in the old windows shattered, scattering shards all over the floor. Everyone dove under whatever surface they could find as they ducked for cover. Bricks from the sidewalls crashed onto the floor, and pieces of ceiling tumbled down.

Joe came running back into the warehouse amid the chaos. "Call for an ambulance! Get the harbor patrol and the fire department! Courtney took the bomb to the end of the pier. I can't see through the fire and smoke!"

Thomas thought the floor was going to give way beneath him. His legs felt like rubber, and his heart lodged in his throat. Rick was by his side in an instant.

"She's dead. I know it." He swiftly turned and grabbed his buddy by the lapels of his jacket, screaming in rage, "You did this to her! You made her go and didn't stop her!"

"Settle down. This is bad, but don't jump to conclusions. You'll be no good to anyone if you can't aid in the search and rescue should we need to."

Thomas's mind flashed from one scenario to another. He needed a drink, a really stiff drink, to calm his nerves. Courtney had to be okay. She'd told him she loved him. If she'd broken her promise and gone off and gotten herself killed…

Sirens roared from the distance, growing louder.

Reggie stood alongside Rick. He turned to the agents helping with the cleanup of the operation. "You've got this contained, Agent Spaulding?"

"Yes, sir."

He redirected his instructions. "We're going to see what we can find out about Agent Stockton. Sam, call the Director."

Sam, who was in the process of calming down a hysterical Hailey, waved his phone in their direction. He had the Director on speed dial and no doubt by the end of the day, Thomas knew his aunt would be in the Hamptons for a full briefing.

Reggie placed a reassuring arm on Thomas's shoulder. Taking out his earpiece, now activated, he eyed Thomas solemnly. "It's going to be rough out there. You can wait here or you can come. Your choice."

"I'm coming. I need to see her."

"Let's roll." Reggie walked off, his earpiece in place, with Rick and Thomas trailing behind. Once the door opened, the hint of morning light showed a scene of mass destruction.

Thomas swallowed hard. Smoke rose from the ashes of the burning boat. Pieces of the fiberglass yacht stretched the entire length of the long pier. But what Thomas zeroed in on was the SAR rescue copter and the divers bobbing in the waters off the end of the pier by the boat launch.

This can't be happening. Divers in the water? That can only mean one thing. She hadn't made it out in time!

"Rick, at the end of the dock. Take a look." Thomas pointed to where he'd been watching the major action taking place. "Get me access. I need to get closer."

"Reggie!" Rick called to the Scotsman who was talking into his earpiece. The man, deep in conversation hadn't heard anyone calling to him.

Without permission to move closer, Thomas darted in and around the massive crowd of rescue workers and responders. Trying not to trip over the sheets of metal in the parking lot, as well as step in the hot spots, he made it to the end of the pier. Just as he arrived, a body in a rescue basket rose from the water. A woman's body, with an arm dangling over the edge, was drawn up and into the waiting helicopter. The divers in the water saluted and the chopper took off in a westerly direction.

"What the hell do you're think you're doing?" Joe had popped up alongside Thomas, looking none too pleased. Reggie and Rick followed suit.

Thomas pointed skyward to the chopper way off in the distance. "Was that her? What's her condition? Is she dead?"

Sam joined the three men, an earpiece dangling over his shoulder. "Your aunt's on her way. They're airlifting Court to Stony Brook. Broken bones and possible internal injuries. Elizabeth said you're to go back to the house and take my chopper from there. Geoff Daniels is driving your parents to the hospital as we speak. The family will congregate together, once we know her condition."

"Then get me out of here. Now!" Thomas had reached the end of his rope.

Rick kept pace with him as he, once more, wove in and out of the debris, trying to make his way back to the nearest police car. "Thomas. My sister's got more guts than anyone I know. She's come back from horrific injuries in the past. Think positive, man. I know I have to."

Piling into the STPD patrol car with Sam and Rick, leaving Joe and Reggie to sort out the information for the necessary briefings and reports for the Agency, Thomas prayed like he'd never prayed in his life. The woman of his dreams, the love of his life, and hopefully, the mother of his children, had to pull through.

Courtney Ellen Stockton had made him a promise. She'd told him she loved him. And that was as good as it could ever get in his book.

* * *

Stony Brook Medical Center
Stony Brook, New York

The Hallock clan had gathered in a private consultation room with Rick, Sam Tanner and Elizabeth, awaiting the medical briefing by the team of doctors in charge of Courtney's care.

Thomas paced the room. It had been two hours since she'd been brought into the Emergency Room. Medical tests and scans took place in rapid fashion, and the family had been escorted off to a private area.

"Thomas, come sit by me," Helen Hallock said, patting the chair next to her. He saw the concerned look on his mother's face and shook his head. Each and every family member had their own way of coping with stress – Thomas paced, his aunt worked 24/7, his mother planned the next wedding in the family.

The door opened. A scrub nurse entered the room, closing the door behind them.

"Elizabeth Hallock?" The nurse read from the clipboard in front of her. "Courtney has you listed as a reference on her HIPAA form as well as her brother, Rick. Could the two of you step outside so the doctors can speak to you?"

Thomas's aunt rose from her chair. "Yes, certainly. Rick, come with me."

Being left out did not sit well with Thomas. "Auntie, I don't understand why you can't share Courtney's information with the rest of us. We're all family. Or soon will be."

On her way to the door, his aunt smiled up at him. "It's the law Rick and I will be back in a moment. Make the rounds and get your parents some coffee from that cart over there. After all, we did pay for this wing of the hospital."

Rick held open the door as his aunt and the nurse exited.

Through the slats in the blinds, Thomas could see both his aunt and Rick listening carefully to what the doctors were saying. Only once did his aunt place her hand on Rick's arm and lean her head on his shoulder. What was that all about?

The doctors and nurse had Rick sign papers and walked away. His aunt and his best friend entered the room, their arms locked tightly together.

"Well? How bad is she hurt? Is she going to be all right?" Thomas had all he could do to maintain his composure.

"I think you should do this, Director." Thomas glimpsed his friend take a handkerchief from his pocket. He wiped a tear from the corner of his eye.

"Oh, dear." Helen, who had been standing, drinking a cup of coffee, sat down in her chair and placed it on the table next to her.

"I think it would be best if everyone made themselves comfortable," Elizabeth informed the group. Everyone did as asked, but Thomas leaned back against the wall nearest to where his mother had taken her seat.

"There's good and bad news. First, let me say, Courtney will make a full recovery. How long that takes will depend on the amount of PT and rehab she has to undertake. She's got a broken collarbone, right arm and left leg that they are going to have to operate and set. Her spleen needs to be removed as it was punctured by something during the blast. But, the doctors are more concerned at the moment, and will not know for some time, whether her uterus was damaged. Things looks okay, but only time will tell." His aunt's eyes fell directly on him. "Thomas, there's a possibility she may not be able to have children."

A collective gasp went around the room. He felt the warmth from his mother's hand reach up and hold his own.

"Auntie, Courtney and I will deal with that when the time comes. Right now just hearing she's going to make a full recovery is music to my ears. I think for us all." There were murmurs in agreement around the room. "When can I see her?"

Rick spoke up. "The doc said only family. The Director and I think you should be the one to go in before they take her up to surgery. It's going to be a long couple of nights."

"Show me the way."

Rick pointed to the door and the nurse waiting outside.

"Give her our love, Thomas," Helen and Robert chimed in unison.

"Will do."

* * *

Courtney's hospital room

Upon entering the room, Thomas couldn't believe the number of machines attached to Courtney's body, each making a different sound, performing a different function.

Standing at her bedside, he looked down upon his Sleeping Beauty. Looking bruised and battered, she still seemed so peaceful, so restful. What she'd gone through, to save him and his family's business, the debt could never be fully repaid.

Sitting in the chair next to the bed, he took her hand in his, his eyes transfixed on her face.

He swallowed the lump in his throat, he swiped at the tears forming in the corner of his eyes. "Courtney, when you wake up, you and I are going to have a long, long talk. No more of playing secret agent woman. I want us to be two people in love with life and each other. Got that? No more bombs, racing through the streets of foreign countries, finding stolen art treasures…oh, yeah. Aunt Elizabeth told me about Positano, I think, just to take my mind off everything.

"I want to grow old with you, sweetheart. Spend our days walking the beach every night holding hands thinking about the joys the next day will hold. We'll travel the world, but this time out in the open, not undercover.

"I want us to be married on the beach just as the sun goes down over the Atlantic and then—"

It was then her hand moved.

"Courtney? Honey?"

Her eyes fluttered open. She was stunning, bruised face and all. She tugged at his hand again. He intertwined his fingers with hers as much as he could without hurting her. She was trying to speak. Bending his head closer to her lips, he could barely make out what she was trying to say.

Finally, she managed to whisper, "Fire…Fireworks!" With great effort she opened her dark eyes wide and smiled up at him. "I want fireworks when the sun goes down. Red, white and blue. Promise me. Perfect for the Fourth of July…"

Her eyes closed, and she drifted back into her drug-induced sleep, the glowing smile still on her face.

He heard a door open and looked to see a nurse and orderly dressed in operating scrubs standing, a waiting look on their face.

"Mr. Hallock. We have to take her up to the operating room. Need to get this fighter back in one piece."

"Of course. She woke up for just a few minutes."

"Good!" The nurse scrawled something on the chart she held in her hand. "The surgeon will be happy to hear that. We'll take it from here."

Thomas didn't want to leave her side, but he nodded in compliance. When he got back to the private reception area, he'd share their news with his family. Mother would get her dream. A daughter-in-law on the Fourth of July!

THE END

Did you enjoy **THE ROMANCE EQUATION?**
Would you like to read more of the series, **Hampton Thoroughbreds?** If so, go to www.dianeculvebooks.com.

Book 1: LOVE ON THE RUN

When Katherine Hallock uses her CIA connections to secure herself in a safe house guarded by Special Agent John Clinton, she thinks life there will be a walk in the park letting the Agency sort out the problems that made her flee Hampton Beach. But John, trusted with his first assignment since creating an international incident in Istanbul, has different plans for the sexy, head strong, determined equine vet. When a series of suspicious events unfold, John is informed his nemesis, Zoya Stalinski, has found him. Can John, who lives every day for love of country, and Katherine, for love of family, unite to take down one of the world's most wanted operatives? Is it possible to find love on the run?

"This is one of those books that grabs your attention within the first five pages and doesn't let it go until the last page. I couldn't put it down! This story takes twists and turns that will keep you guessing until the very end."
Amazon Customer Review

BOOK 2: HURRICANE MEGAN

Matthew Hallock is known in Hampton Beach for two passions: one-night stands and his stake in the Sunfish Beach Club. When Megan Spears lands the job as his chief lifeguard, he is drawn to her from the minute she blows her whistle. But Megan has no time for men. She's on a mission – literally. And even if she did have time, in her book opposites don't attract.

Can two people from totally different walks of life find the common ground needed to walk hand in hand into the future under a Hampton sunset?

"This is a perfect beach book. Written by a real Hampton local, so it is full of authentic color. A fun read for the beach, pool or backyard. Put your mind in neutral and enjoy the ride!"
Amazon Customer Review

HAMPTON COFFEE COMPANY

On a trip home to Westhampton Beach several summers ago, Diane stumbled upon a "new" coffee shop in town…and the rest is history. HCC is one of her "must-go-to" places on her checklist when she heads to the East. End.

The Hampton Coffee Company is a must-stop for not only the author, but for locals, tourists and many celebrities. The Company started in Water Mill more than twenty-years ago. There are also location in Westhampton Beach and Southampton.

Diane is most grateful for Hampton Coffee Company to allow her to set several of the scenes of her new book, *The Romance Equation*, in its shop in Southampton. As she types this thank you, her mind is imagining the pastry shelf filled with every kind of Danish possible. And, yes, she has tasted many, along with sipping the best coffee she's ever had. She encourages you to visit their website store, shop and taste in person or like them on Facebook.

Hampton Coffee Company must be doing something right given the awards and recognitions received. They are regularly featured in Dan's Papers, Hampton's Magazine, and the

Southampton Press. HCC set an all time record for five wins in a year – best cappuccino, coffee, breakfast spot, coffee shop and waiter!

So guess, where Diane is heading on her next trip home? You got it! Hampton Coffee Company! "Hamptons Hot Spot"... Put it on YOUR checklist as a place to grab something to eat when you're in town. Remember the locations: Water Mill, Southampton and Westhampton Beach.

ABOUT THE AUTHOR

Diane Culver was born and raised in Westhampton Beach. She spent her first twenty-one years soaking up life in the Hamptons. After a career as an award winning mathematics teacher spanning thirty-one plus years, Diane retired and resides in a small community in Central New York on the outskirts of Syracuse.

Diane is probably the only person (except for the crazy ski people) who looks forward to the snow piling up outside her window. It's a perfect excuse to pour a cup of Earl Grey tea, cozy up on the sofa by the fireplace, and work on her next book. Contact her at dianeculverbooks@gmail.com or visit her website: www.dianeculverbooks.com to find out what's up and coming in the series: *Hampton Thoroughbreds*.

SPECIAL THANK YOUS

Diane would like to extend a very special thank you to the following people: Jessica Lewis, who helped format the book for publishing and helped create publicity posters for book signings. Contact Jessica at (www.authorslifesaver.com). Several writing chapters have been invaluable in her journey in writing: the Central New York Romance Writers Chapter of the RWA (www.cnyromancewriters.com) and the Long Island Romance Writers (www.lirw.org). Her friends on Long Island keep her in touch with what goes on in the Hamptons when she can't be there to enjoy the sand, surf and long walks on the beach by Jetty 4.

The Romance Equation was edited by Gina Ardito. Gina is the owner of Excellence in Editing and a hybrid author of more than twenty contemporary and paranormal romances. For information about her editing services see her website: http://excellenceinediting.com. For information about her books, you can connect with her at www.ginaardito.com.